Never That Far

Never That Far

CAROL LYNCH WILLIAMS

SHADOW
MOUNTAIN

Sunburst design © Shutterstock/21kompot

Visit us at ShadowMountain.com

Library of Congress Cataloging-in-Publication Data

Names: Williams, Carol Lynch, author.
Title: Never that far / Carol Lynch Williams.
Description: Salt Lake City, Utah : Shadow Mountain, [2018] | Summary: "When twelve-year-old Libby's grandfather dies of a heart attack, it's up to her—and his spirit—to find a way to help her father overcome his grief and for their family to find peace."—Provided by publisher.
Identifiers: LCCN 2017040902 | ISBN 9781629724096 (hardbound : alk. paper)
Subjects: | CYAC: Fathers and daughters—Fiction. | Grief—Fiction. | Grandfathers—Fiction. | Spirits—Fiction. | LCGFT: Fiction.
Classification: LCC PZ7.W65588 Ng 2018 | DDC [Fic]—dc23
LC record available at https://lccn.loc.gov/2017040902

Printed in the United States of America
Edwards Brothers Malloy, Ann Arbor, MI

10 9 8 7 6 5 4 3 2 1

To my *daddy, Richard Thomas Lynch*

Chapter One

What you doing, girl?" Daddy said when the burying was done.

I stood on the unpainted block fence and looked off East.

The Lake Mary Church of Christ preacher, Melinda Burls, had said the dead go East. Couldn't give me a reason when I asked her why.

"They just do, Libby," she said, and with one finger, she touched the top of my head like she was baptizing me all over again. Then she tapped her stomach where a long string of fake pearl beads ended up. "I know it right here."

"In your belly?" I squinched my eyes.

The beads swung over her scrawny self. I felt a little sorry for her. But not *too* much.

"In my heart," she said.

I gave a nod and looked away from her face. I stared straight into the sun for as long as I could, just because. Then I glanced back at her. For a moment, she seemed to glow. "Your heart's awful low," I said, feeling mean on accounta the circumstances. "You might need a operation to get that fixed."

"It's Jesus' heart," she said, like she didn't hear me. She looked off toward Daddy, who stood alone, staring at his shoe-tops. Then she licked her lips. "This is a day you won't hardly forget, now will you? September third, in the year of our Lord, nineteen hundred and sixty-seven. No, sirree, you won't be forgetting today."

"No, ma'am," I said. She was right about that.

I stomped off, mad. Didn't want to hear another word about it. No more Jesus stuff. No more "in the year of our Lord" stuff. No more religion. Not right now.

"Don't seem right," I said, kicking through the dirt road on my way free of the morning. My sneakers was like tight red flowers. Behind me the funeral broke up. I could hear the high rise of bawling. Car doors slamming shut. Daddy, I knew, would be looking for me, Preacher Burls stuck close to his side.

I plowed on, my head bent so it led the way.

"Don't seem fair *she* got Jesus' heart." I kicked at an old Campbell's soup can, rusted in the middle where it was bent. It flew into a high tangle of dried-out ditch weeds.

Life ain't meant to be fair popped into my head. Preacher Burls's words when Daddy asked "Why?" I could almost see his lips making them words. "Why now? Why us? Why again?"

It's what he asked when we found Grampa. Almost gone, hanging on to life and to the yellow tablecloth from the kitchen.

"If there was hearts to spare," I said, my cotton dress sticking to my back and under my arms, "Burls shouldn't have got it."

Especially seeing the way Grampa had died. His own heart giving up, puttering out. His last words to me from where he lay on the floor was about the lake. It seemed to me that if anybody needed Jesus' heart, it would have been Grampa, the best man ever born this side of the Lamb.

Burls seemed healthy enough without taking the extras for herself.

"But life ain't fair," I said. And when I heard cars coming up on me, I stepped into the weeds, down into that deep ditch, back up the other side, and into an orange grove, where the fruit was young and still just hard green balls.

I made my way home. Didn't nobody come looking for me. Not that I woulda took their help. Still, someone *mighta* had him some manners and come searching. It was Daddy's doing. He probably told them I needed my time. He probably said, "That girl is almost thirteen going on almost forty-four and she needs her time." He probably said, "That girl don't need no one."

And then, like all them people knew what he said was truth, everybody nodded. And left me to walk in the wet fire of the Florida day. Loneliness stretched out like a path in front of me.

Through the grove I went, hot. The late morning air was tired and rested on me like it needed a lift somewhere. The trees, waxy-leaved, hid the sun some. My shoes filled with sand.

"This all my grampa's," I said. 'Course there was no one to answer.

"No," I said. "Now, this all mine and Daddy's."

A mile or two more and I'd be back home. But I wouldn't stop there.

Not a lick of breeze stepped up to cool things off.

I paused and leaned into a Parson Brown orange tree. Squeezed my eyes shut and walked into the branches until I was to the narrow trunk. I breathed deep the smell of oranges and dirt. The scent made me tear right up. Then I wrapped my arms around a limb and whispered so only the tree could hear, "You know Grampa thought Parson Browns was the sweetest orange of all. You do good this year. You give us lots of fruit to show you loved Grampa, too."

A knot of tears clogged my throat. For a moment I thought *I* might die, my chest hurt so much. More heart business running in the Lochewood family. Broken hearts everywhere.

I let go of the tree and dropped to my knees. Three tears sneaked out and I wiped them away fast. My hands was dirty. Gray from my walk and the petting of this Parson Brown.

"Grampa," I said, "you done me wrong."

I hadn't been in the kitchen since that morning.

I remembered me and Daddy running into Grampa, who'd called out once, "Libby?"

My name—a question.

Then I'd heard this *thunk* from where I sat in my room, drawing a picture of me with one eye using an old purple crayon. Been bored up to that moment.

I'd run, my heart pounding so I felt it in the base of my skull. Met Daddy in the hall. We'd bumped into each other—he'd knocked me into the golden pine wall on accident—but I'd caught ahold of my balance.

Funny, how we knew.

Grampa on the floor, clutching the tablecloth. Ice water spreading out in a puddle beside him. The glass right there by his ear, not even broke.

"Libby?"

Daddy and me, we both fell to our knees. Later I found the bruises from that kneeling.

"Pop? What is it?" Daddy's voice was like a girl's. Thin. Watery.

Grampa didn't answer. His eyes rolled back into his head till only the whites showed.

Daddy got up. Went running barefoot—*thump thump thump*—into the hall where the phone sat on the low table. I heard him dialing.

I took Grampa's free hand in my own. Big old fingers. Warm and knuckle-hard. Bent some.

"Get up," I said, pulling. But he wouldn't budge. "Let me get you up."

Daddy yelled for help in the other room.

Grampa said, "I left you something, Libby." His eyes gone white.

"Did you bump yourself?" I said. But I knew all along it was worse than that. "Let me help you sit."

"Listen to me good," he said. "And believe."

I dipped my head till my face rested on his. "I'm listening." That was the first time I cried, tears splatting on his neck.

"I left you something in the lake."

"You didn't need to do that," I said.

But Grampa didn't answer.

Now, on my knees again, in the heat of the funeral morning, I watched black ants crawl in the sand. And when I cried, I aimed my tears at them, hitting four. Then I got myself up and walked the rest of the way, right past our house, and deep into the property where the lake is.

I sat out there all day.

Took my dress off at one point and let the sun cook on my shoulders and down my back around my training bra. I edged my way to the water and then scooted in, soaking my undies to the waist. The minnows came to nibble at me, but I wouldn't let them.

I was alone now.

All alone.

Daddy might be at home, but he wasn't really there. And the truth was, I'd need someone now that my grandfather was gone.

When the sun settled down for the night, and the mosquitoes came out for dinner, I got myself dressed again and went on up to the house.

To where my grampa wasn't.

Chapter Two

It was 2:35 in the A.M. when Grampa woke me. I saw that clear on the round face of my illuminated clock. Pale, shiny green numbers. Two and seven pointed out with slender sticks of glow-in-the-dark light.

He said, "Libby?"

I sat up in bed and looked around my room.

"Daddy?"

"No, it's me," he said. "It's your grandfather."

"Grampa?"

I took in a deep breath. Had his dying all been a dream? Was I dreaming now? I squeezed my eyes shut, then opened them wide. "You really here?"

He gave a nod that sent light shooting to the mirror on my dresser. "I am," he said.

I had some thinking to do. All about my grampa. There was his falling on the floor. There was his white-eyed stare. There was his funeral. And now he sat on the foot of my bed? My heart gave a jump big as a frog can make. I wasn't scared. More happy for another opportunity to be with him. Still there was things to be found out. Even if this was a dream.

"I thought you was gone—you know, East."

"East?" Grampa said. He shook his head. A glow came off his skin like light shining on a body after it's been in the rain. "Why you think I been off East? Nothing there but the Atlantic."

"Well, sure," I said, "but . . ." I leaned in close. Was he a ghost? Or was I cuckoo? I kept my eyes wide. Watching. Staring.

I tried again. "Preacher Burls, she said—"

Grampa stopped me short with a laugh. Sparks of light flew into the black air of my room.

"Preacher Burls don't know her backside from the Book of Matthew." He laughed again. More sparks. "Things ain't all what she thinks. Not a lot of what *anyone* alive thinks."

I wanted to reach out and touch Grampa, but thought better of it. What if it burned? What if it killed me? Worse yet, what if my touching him made Grampa leave—or woke me from this dream?

We sat quiet a minute. From outside came the voices of frogs singing rain-songs and crickets calling out to friends.

Grampa settled on the edge of the bed, not even making an indentation on the sheet. His glow flared, then came down soft around the edges once he seemed comfortable.

"You done what I said?" he asked after a while.

I stared at him until my eyeballs burned. He seemed real enough. I give myself a pinch in the dark. It smarted. Seemed I *was* awake.

"What do you mean?"

"You been searching out to the lake for what I left ya?"

I blinked, cooling my whole face. "Naw, Grampa. I been down there today, though. Sat there some. Just breathing." I had a pink sunburn on my face and shoulders and back to prove it.

"That's all right, I guess," Grampa said. He moved up the bed to where I sat. The good smells of bacon with a rind and coffee with sweetened condensed milk came with him.

"You leaving?" I said. Pain, like a splinter, hit me in the chest. Grampa's face seemed clear, younger. Not so wrinkled, not so tired. His eyes were see-through green.

"For now," he said and set his lips to my cheek. The sting of sunburn was gone at his touch. "But I'll be back. You go on to sleep now. I'm gonna check in on your daddy."

I lay back. Pulled the sheet to my chin.

I didn't think I could sleep a wink, that's for sure. Not seeing what had happened to me. Not seeing what was to happen with Daddy. This was exciting news.

Preacher Burls was right about one thing even if she got her directions all mixed up. People *did* live after dying.

"You'll be back?"

"Of course. The dead ain't never that far from the living."

"Pinkie promise?" I held my little finger out to Grampa. And just like when he was alive, he grabbed ahold of it with his little finger and answered, "Pinkie promise, Libby-girl."

Then he stood and walked through the wall, trailing green and white and blue.

I was asleep before the light faded away.

"Well?" I said to Daddy at the table that morning, when the sun sat high in the sky. We'd slept in. Daddy, 'cause he was tormented with missing *his* daddy. Me, 'cause I'd been up late, talking. My heart moved with happiness. I could feel it in my wrists.

Daddy sat quiet, saying nothing, like I wasn't there.

"Well?" I said again. I gave the table a *thump, thump* with my hands.

"Well, what?" Daddy said. He pushed around eggs over-easy with a piece of toast. He needed a shave. It seemed his hair had fought a battle and lost. He wouldn't look straight at me.

"Did you talk to Grampa last night?"

I chowed down my breakfast. Now that I knew I'd be getting visits I wasn't too worried about the day passing. Plus there was the lake to look forward to. Finding whatever was there.

"Not sure what you mean," Daddy said, letting out a long sigh. He appeared all wore out. Beat up. "I thought about him some." Daddy's eyes filled with tears. Eyes like his own daddy's. Like mine.

He set the toast down.

"But did you *talk* to him?"

"No."

"He didn't stop in for a visit?" I quit chewing. Outside a dog barked twice. I could smell Daddy's coffee.

"Girl!" Daddy's hand slapped the table with a *pop.* "Why you doing this to me? Can't you see I'm all tore up inside?"

"Yes, sir," I said. "I can see that real good. But . . ." I was on the way to saying "But he mentioned he would stop in to your room on his way outta mine" when I caught myself.

For whatever reason Daddy *hadn't* had a chance to speak to his father. Why should I make him feel bad that *I* had?

"I know for sure he loves us both," I said instead.

I felt shook up, unsteady, that Daddy hadn't seen Grampa. The happiness leaked right out of me. I could almost feel it seeping from my pores.

Daddy stood and left the room like his tail was on fire and I was kerosene. He didn't even glance back.

"Oh," I said.

In slow motion, I finished eating by myself. Then I cleaned up some, so no ants or roaches would come in from outside. I swept the floor where Grampa had laid, lying in his death spot for a few minutes. Then I shook out that yellow tablecloth, tossing away the crumbs we'd spread on it.

At last I went to my room to get ready.

First thing I saw the sunburn was gone. My skin was pale as ever, 'ceptin' on closer investigation I saw the print. It looked like a kiss, there on my cheek. Pink-colored.

"Why, thank you, Grampa," I said into the air. Just in case he was listening. "Now anytime I need a reminder of your visit, alls I got to do is peek in the mirror."

Grampa didn't show hide nor hair, but that was okay with me. I knew firsthand he was fine. And I knew, first-hand, that the dead ain't never that far from the living. If I needed him, I was sure he'd come to me.

I packed up a brown paper bag of lunch. I made a egg salad sandwich, pulled out brownies left by some church ladies' auxiliary, and poured lemonade into a plaid thermos bottle.

The phone rang and I went in the other room to get it.

"Hello?" I said.

"This is Melinda," Preacher Burls said. "How's your daddy doing, little Libby?"

"Almost thirteen ain't little," I said. I licked the side of my hand where I had spilt lemonade in the lunch-making process. "Daddy's laying up in the bed, with a cold cloth stuck to his forehead. Cried all night, I bet."

Preacher Burls let out a gasp. "I best get on over there," she said. "There is a lamb in distress. The shepherdess must see to her flock." She cleared her throat, and I could almost see her playing with them beads like she does when she comes by to bring us dinner. She ain't a bad cook, not that her food has put much meat on her own bones.

"Ain't *Jesus* the Shepherd?" I said. I was still feeling mean, though most of the time me and her get along good. "Just wondering."

Preacher Burls has a right keen way of ignoring anyone she wants. Like the questions in church she doesn't know the answers to. Or me when I'm bothering her. She did that now. "Tell your daddy I'm on my way to visit him."

"I will," I said.

"That's a good girl," she said.

Before she could hang up, I said, "Preacher Burls? You remember how you said the dead go East?"

"I reckon I do," she said. She let out a sigh. I wasn't sure if it was 'cause she was anxious to get on over to our place or else feeling happy that I listened to her for once.

"You ever think the only thing out there is the ocean?"

She was quiet a moment.

"Bye now," I said, and hung right up.

Chapter Three

The start of school was two weeks away. The thought made my toes ache. What a time for Grampa to choose to die. He *coulda* waited till I was settled in class. *Coulda* waited till he had walked me to the bus stop a few times, holding my hand tight in his. *Coulda* waited till I'd done my school supplies shopping. My heart squeezed at my throat. I remembered him in my room, remembered all that light, remembered my pink kiss. I took a few deep breaths, and a bit of sadness drained away.

I had me two weeks to find the treasure in the lake. Two. That was as long as my days would be free.

"Libby Jefferson Lochewood," I said, cruising off

toward the water. My momma, long gone now, chose to name me after my grandfather. Her father-in-law. Jefferson is his first name. I mean, was. *Was.* "You ain't got a lotta time."

I hate school. I hate climbing on that bus, playing the fashion game with the kids in my class, looking at the new ways girls stare at boys. It's like I am on the outside of a fish tank looking in at everybody else. Or maybe it's me that is the fish. Who knows?

Don't get me wrong. I have friends. Both girls and boys. But I liked it better with Grampa, walking through the groves, lighting the smudge pots in the winter to keep trees from freezing, planting rows of vegetable seeds in our garden. I didn't want to be tied to a desk, sand on the floor scratching beneath my shoes, reciting the times tables or the capitals of the states or saying what president was born where and when.

Ouch.

There was that sadness again. I hoped Grampa'd show up more than just the once. I hoped he'd keep that pinkie promise of his.

Daddy hadn't seen him.

Why not?

Had he looked past Grampa the way he looked past me?

What if Grampa never came back?

"Don't you be thinking that way," I said, loud and nasty to myself, walking fast before the sun got too high. Though it was only ten in the morning, it was right hot already, and I felt tears come up. The kind that sting and make your nose burn like you've taken a tumble under a salty wave. "He *is* coming back. He ain't gone for good."

A nagging feeling sat in my head like a nesting bird. Only this wasn't something small. This was a eagle-sized bird. And I needed to send it flapping away.

"You were here last night, right?" I kept staring at the ground, just in case Grampa didn't show. That way I wouldn't have to see. "You wasn't just my imagination?"

Grampa *mighta* showed his face but I never looked up. Still, I felt all right inside, smoothed over like cake icing. I felt like maybe he watched over me. The feeling gave me courage.

"Grampa," I said, confident. "You lead where you want me to go."

While Florida is flat as a new frying pan, Grampa's property—I mean, *our* property—slants down till it winds up where the lake sits. Acres of land and water. White sand paths lead everywhere, some wide enough to drive a car down, others just for your feet. The place is covered with live oaks with Spanish moss tumbling from the limbs. Pines that have attracted rattlesnakes as big around as my arm. Bushes of every variety. Not much grass grows on account of how crowded out the sun is by trees.

The lake is a good twenty minutes away from the house on foot. Straight through the woods. The air as heavy as a sponge full of water.

At the edge of the woods, the trees cleared, leaving nothing but low-cut grass. I stopped and stared at that lake with a new eye, a trained eye. Trained for what, I wasn't sure. But I stared at the place for a reason. And having a reason very near made me a detective like Sherlock Holmes.

Making my hand a hat brim, I shaded my face and stared at the promise of the lake. The water was choppy from a wind that seemed to stop blowing as soon as it met the sand. At least *I* couldn't feel it from where I stood.

Things was cleared up for entertaining near the water. Grasses cut back, a picnic table, a wider sand path. A old brick patio was built a hundred yards from the lip of the lake. Grampa'd put all that together long before I was born. Three Adirondack chairs sat in a circle, a pot-belly grill the center of things—all there for barbequing chicken covered in Gramma's secret sauce. All there for me and Grampa, and for Daddy when he chose. My heart stopped beating a few moments and I thought of the three of us turning into two. For sure we weren't coming out here for a good long while. Not together. It hurt my heart like a hard pinch.

"Take a deep breath," I said. "Keep looking for whatever it is Grampa wants you to find."

A old raft floated on barrels right near the shore, swelling up and down, anchored with a cinder block. I'd laid out on that raft, roasting in the sun, plenty a times. From the limb of a lone oak, one that reached into the sky like a child holding her arms out, Grampa had hung me a tire swing.

I did as I told myself and pulled in a deep breath, smelling the sun, and wandered on down to the shore.

"Libby? Libby?"

My name echoed out over the water, and my heart gave a thump.

"Grampa?" I turned to find him this time, to see his shiny skin, to see the sparks fly. Would he glow in the full light of day? But it wasn't Grampa at all, just Bobby Myers from down the road a piece and his twin sister, Martha.

Not sure why they are called twins other than they share a birthday. Bobby, he's short, and Martha, she stretches up taller than anyone in our sixth-grade class. And, man, she is smart, too. Smarter than everyone, even

Jeffrey Scott, who wears glasses thick as a Coke-bottle bottom.

Neither Bobby nor Martha, nor their momma and daddy, go to the Lake Mary Church of Christ with us. They don't go to a church at all. Preacher Burls says the whole lot of them is heathens. I think that's why I like them so much.

"Hey you," Martha called, and she laughed, her voice winding down to me.

"Hey you, too," I said right back. "What are you doing out here?"

Bobby took off running, his feet flying over the sand, leaping over nothing, blond hair flapping in the breeze. He stopped right in front of me. Martha came on down slow. They were both tan as nuts.

"We found this lake at the beginning of summer," Bobby said. "Been here a few times. You can see right to the bottom, you know that?"

I nodded. 'Course I knew that, seeing how this was our lake. And I told him as much.

"Been swimming in this ol' place since before I could walk," I said, which was the real truth, every word.

"Whachu doing now?" Bobby said.

"Looking for treasure," I said. No need to lie. I could use their help. Why, I'd even share what we found.

"What kind of treasure?" he said. Martha came to a stop next to her brother.

I shrugged. "Don't know yet."

He nodded, hands on his hips like he was already investigating.

"Then why you looking?" said Martha. "Maybe it's one big waste of time." Her chocolate-colored hair hung long down her back, way past her waist. I could see a rat's nest right in the middle of it when she looked around the property.

"Maybe," I said. I gave a shrug. "But a treasure's a good thing to have, and I felt like searching."

"Supposing there is one—where *might* it be?" Martha said.

"Out thataway." I pointed by nodding my head toward the lake.

"You got a map?" Martha said. "All treasures got maps."

Bobby stared at me, his eyes the shade of a old mushroom.

"Nope," I said. "But I don't need one."

"You looking for gold bullion?" Martha said. "Everyone in Florida knows the Spaniards buried gold pieces everywhere all over this state. And near water, too, though I never heard tell it was near *lake* water."

She hitched up her underwear by grabbing ahold of it through her dress and pulling straight up.

"Ain't got no idea where or how or why, just know it's waiting," I said. "And if the two of you want to help me, you'd be welcome." Saying the words made me feel generous. And why not? I was sure there was enough to share.

"We might end up rich," Bobby said. He grinned at me. One front tooth had a chip in it. He'd gotten that chip when Denny O'Rourke called Bobby a liar and then whopped him in the face during a school bus fight. Both boys had to walk home that day. It was a ugly memory and made me sick to my stomach still. Especially thinking how Bobby'd hocked up part of his tooth and a wad of spit and blood next to my sandal right before tearing into Denny and busting his butt. Bobby was a good friend to have on your side, he sure was.

And cute, too. Not that I woulda told nobody.

Bobby kept on grinning. "I'll do it," he said. "And you don't have to pay me no gold. Unless a-course you want to."

"I would want to," I said, squinting in the sun. "Fair is fair."

"Then," said Martha, moving up close to me and Bobby, "let's get to work."

Chapter Four

What we did first was push out into the lake in Grampa's rowboat. It's an old wood thing with a bright red coat of paint. On the side, in small white letters with a echo of black, is my name, *Libby*, in slanty letters.

"Since we're looking for gold," Bobby said, removing his shirt and setting it on the bow of the boat, "I think we should stare into the water till we see it." All of him was tan, tan, tan.

"You kidding me?" Martha said.

"No, I ain't kidding you," Bobby said. "Peer into that there water, Martha."

She did. "So?"

"It's clear as if it comes from the spigot in the kitchen. We can see to the bottom. Any gold down there, we'll know it sure."

"That ain't my point, brother Bobby." Martha calls him that on account of she is eighteen minutes older than him. She passed me a smile.

"Then what is, sister Sue?" Bobby grinned at me, turning so I could see his face. His blond hair flopped into his eyes.

I settled into the bottom of the boat to listen to the argument. Not having a brother or sister of my own—though I more than wished I did—made this interesting, though a itchiness of hurry crawled down my back. Knowing these two, though, it wasn't good to interrupt. Just had to wait the disagreement out.

"Look at the size of this place." Martha gestured with both hands, sweeping around the lake. "It's gotta be a hundred miles big. You want to paddle this thing, having us gawk over the edge? It'll take forever. And I ain't got a forever, don't cha know."

She's right. Our lake is huge.

"You got a better way?" Bobby didn't sound mad. In fact, in all the years I've known him, I've only seen him fit to be tied a few times. And never at Martha. "That water is like glass. And we ain't got no scuba gear, so that won't work. If there's gold down there, the sun will catch on it and send a beam straight up to us. Like a beacon. Like in *Star Trek*."

"Oh, yeah," I said from my resting position. "*Star Trek*." A beam of light like in the show sure would be exciting to see.

Bobby was right, too. At least about the lake being clear to the bottom.

"There's gotta be a better way," Martha said.

I don't know how long we floated, waiting for Martha to come up with some idea, but it seemed a lengthy, hot time.

Bobby asked about Grampa, told me how sorry he was my grandfather was gone. We both agreed at the sadness of death.

"When my nana passed on," Bobby said, his legs slung over the side of the boat while Martha sat on the only board seat, thinking hard, her chin resting in both hands, "I like to have passed on, too. At least that's what it felt like. Me and Martha cried and cried for I don't know how long."

"Months," Martha said, barely parting her lips to let the word out. Her eyes were shut, contemplating, it seemed.

"I didn't think I'd ever get over her going. We was best of friends, the three of us."

"I know what that's like," I said, whispering.

"I know you do," Bobby said. "I seen you with your grampa. You was bosom buddies."

I bent close to him. Leaned toward his ear. I smelled pennies. "You ever seen your nana? After she was gone, I mean?"

Bobby moved closer, till we touched shoulders. "Whatchu mean?"

"She ever visit you once she passed on?" My face burned from his touch. A bit of missing-Grampa sadness came into my chest, right where my heart beat hard.

"Naw, Libby," Bobby said, real sad-like. He reached down and gave my finger a squeeze. "Once they're gone, they're gone."

Martha busted out with a "I got it."

I looked out over the water in the direction my house sat, then back to Martha.

"What we do is let Bobby row us around the lake and you and me, Libby, we look for reflections of gold."

"Good idea," Bobby said. "Glad you thought of it."

We floated around in the boat till our stomachs told us, "Go on home." We stayed in the boat, but my lunch wasn't enough to satisfy the three of us.

Bobby licked egg salad off his thumb. "You know, I read this story 'bout a kid just our age."

"No you don't," Martha said. "No stories."

Bobby ignored her. Turned his full attention to me. "He wasn't the smartest kid in the world. You'll see that in a minute."

"You better tell him to shut up," Martha said. She wiped at her mouth with the back of her hand. "I mean it."

I looked between the two of them.

"Anyways, his momma never cooked him a meal. Never. I read this in the paper."

"Stop him, Libby," Martha said.

"Why?" I said.

"You're gonna be sorry."

"Martha, shut up and let me tell y'all what happened." Martha looked away from both of us, disgusted.

"He decides to cook himself some oatmeal. And he does. But when it's time to put on sugar, he cain't find any. So he goes on out to the shed. He finds this jar with this white stuff in it that looks like powdered sugar."

"What was he looking in the shed for?" I said.

"See what I mean," Bobby said and tapped his forehead.

I did not see what he meant, but I kept quiet.

"It was rat poison," he said. "Sprinkled it all over his oatmeal. Put in milk and butter and lots of rat poison."

"No, he did not." I covered my mouth with my hand.

"So his momma hears him screaming. She comes

running in. He's wiggling all over the floor like he's trying to get away from the pain. There's puke and blood everywhere and—"

"Shut up, I say," Martha said.

"Yeah," I said. "I don't think I want to hear anymore." My stomach felt stretched out and thin.

"He didn't die."

"Don't care."

"The story has a happy ending."

"You know it doesn't," Martha said to me.

"He lived."

"Can you make him stop?" I said.

Martha shook her head.

"He's just paralyzed from the bottom lip down."

In all our looking, we didn't see nothing but perch and catfish. And we hadn't even covered a piece of the lake. My neck grew a crick in it so sharp I wondered if I'd ever straighten it out. Maybe I'd go to school and be called "Crookneck," like I was a squash or something.

"Useless idea you had, Bobby," Martha said, when he'd rowed us back to shore.

Bobby said nothing, just squinted at the both of us.

"I don't see how we're ever gonna find a treasure," she said.

I kept my lips shut tight. With or without Martha and Bobby, I'd find what Grampa had left for me. Might be more fun, the three of us looking, but if I had to do it alone, I would. I'd get what I was sent for. Whatever it was.

Martha stretched her back out, bending this way and that. Bobby picked at a blister in the center of his palm that he'd gotten rowing.

"Tomorrow, then?" Martha said. She tilted her head to the side, waiting for my answer.

"You coming back?" I said.

"'Course," said Bobby.

At home, Daddy talked to Preacher Burls. I caught them sitting in the living room. It seemed like they were praying, the two of them, heads bent together, her long black hair falling forward. I thought of me and Bobby on the boat and him holding onto my finger.

"Lunch is on the table, girl," Daddy said, when I'd looked them over.

"Uh-huh," I said.

"Now Jesus, He wants me to . . ." I heard Preacher Burls say.

I got out of there quick.

"Libby?"

I sat up in bed like I was attached to a spring and glanced at the clock—2:35. Just like before.

"I'm here, Grampa."

"Come to check on you, girl."

"That's so nice of you, Grampa." I meant it, too. Love fell over me like a sheet. My best friend was back again.

He settled on the bed. I could see his skin was younger-looking. I pushed back the covers and moved closer to him. He glowed when I got nearer. Whiter more to the edges. "Where you been all day?" I said.

"I been gone only one day?" His voice sounded surprised.

I nodded. "Only one."

"Sure seems longer than that."

"Sure does," I said. And I meant it.

"I been busy," Grampa said. "Checked in on your gramma. Looked in on your momma."

My eyes went wide in the dark. "You did?" I moved a bit nearer, still worried at touching him. "My momma?"

"Oh, yeah. And with lots others, too. Had a little reunion. All us together, including my boys that died before your daddy was big. Did some loud laughing, some guitar playing." He put his arm around my shoulder, and I felt the buzz of his glow every place he touched me.

"Guitar playing, too?"

"Yes-sirree-Bob."

This close to Grampa, I could smell grapes. And tangerines, too. "You can do that?" Repeating them words made me miss our evenings at home together. Me at Grampa's feet, leaning against his knee. Daddy sipping a cold Bud, resting on the sofa and staring off into space. Grampa singing songs from church and strumming his old guitar.

"Oh, yeah. Lotsa music. Lotsa warm thoughts and good doings. Some bitterness, too. But not where I am."

"Grampa," I said, my voice a whisper. "Grampa, I love you. I love you so much. Thank you for visiting with me."

"You think I'd leave you all alone? Naw, that ain't the way it's supposed to be, Libby. Family is family forever. And for now, we're together."

I thought a minute. "Could you do me a favor?" I said.

Grampa squeezed me and the light bursting around us reminded me of a chrysanthemum. "You know I can."

A bit a shyness came into my heart. "Will ya say hi to Momma for me? You know, if you see her again?"

"Why, Libby, you know I will."

I nodded and snuggled into his side that was warm like a fire.

In the morning, when I woke up, he was gone.

Chapter Five

Daddy didn't get up the next day.

"What're you doing?" I said to him. I waited at his door, looking in the room. It was dark in there, except around the windows where day pushed past the edges of the heavy curtains.

"I'm in the bed with the door shut for a reason," he said. "I *was* sleeping." He sounded grumpy.

"It's time to eat," I said. "It's almost ten in the A.M."

"And why you telling me this?" Daddy sounded like I ate something he'd saved back in the fridge.

"The day's done begun." My voice was whiny. I kicked at the floor with the toe of my old tennis shoe that squeezed my foot. These shoes was too small. It was high time I got new ones. Especially seeing how school was starting in less than two weeks.

But.

But Grampa was dead. And, well, I wasn't ready to give these old things up. He bought them for me at the start of summer. Picked them out and brung them home in a blue Keds box.

"For you," he had said.

I'd been happy to stay barefoot, though I didn't tell him so. Seeing his face looking smiley like it had, I'd taken them shoes.

"Thank you, Grampa."

He'd said, "Libby, you look right pretty in red. And them shoes is gonna make your feet like a movie star's."

I'd worn them only three times that summer.

And every day since he fell in the kitchen. Including to his funeral.

Now Daddy said, "I'm staying in bed, girl, and I ain't getting out for one week."

"Why's that?" Even though I knew, I asked him anyways.

"Why's that?" Daddy's voice didn't break the glass in the windows, but I was sure I heard the panes rattle, it rumbled out that loud. "Why's that? My father is dead. I need to recover. Just like when my mother passed. And when your momma went on. I am going to learn to feel better right here in the dark."

"I see," I said. But I didn't move out of the doorway. Kept on standing and kicking.

I heard Daddy flop around in the bed. "You may not believe it, but he was my friend, too. We was close. Working the groves together. Playing guitar and singing."

In my memory there was a bit of that. My daddy and grampa making music in the living room. Them laughing together. Cutting up.

And it is the truth the two of them worked every bit of our land together.

"Girl." Daddy's voice was tired. I could almost imagine him rubbing at his eyes the way he does when he's wore out from a day in the groves, packing or spraying or managing the migrant workers. "Ain't you got better things to do than look in at me?"

"I guess." I gave a shrug though I knew he couldn't see me.

"Then get on with it."

I stood more still than before.

"What?"

I drug a deep breath into my lungs. Still my voice came out in a whisper. And a ragged one at that. "Ain't you seen him yet?"

Daddy was quieter than minnows at your feet. "Hey," he said after a long minute. "You okay, girl?"

"'Course," I said.

He was silent a good long time, like maybe he was weighing what to say. Then I heard him roll over.

"You need to rest, too. Go on and get into your own bed for a while."

I'm not sure what I wanted from him, what I had hoped Daddy would say. Maybe, "Come on over here, girl, and let me give you a hug. I know you are beat up from sadness." Something. But not to send me away like that.

I stood quiet in his doorway a minute more. Daddy didn't make another sound.

"All right then," I said.

In my room, I cried till my head hurt. Not just for Grampa being gone, but for my daddy and me being so alone. Then I turned over and slept.

"Hey, Libby!"

It was Bobby's voice, sounding through the house. "You coming out here or not? I been waiting hours to go you-know-whatting."

I crawled from bed, my head full of sand. Then I tiptoed out of my room and ran through the house to the screened-in porch. Bobby stood right there, his face pressed into the screen so that his nose looked flat.

"Hey, you," he said, grinning.

"Hey," I said. I squinted against the light, then touched at my hair some. Did I look like something spit out on the road waiting to get run over?

"You look fine," Bobby said like he knew my thoughts. He didn't have a shirt on. And that boy was skinny all over. Skinny arms. Skinny legs. Skinny ol' neck.

"J'eat yet?" I said.

He nodded.

"Well, I ain't, and I gotta before we get to work."

He nodded again. "All right."

"Where's Martha?" I glanced out to the yard. A mockingbird let out a call. I could smell the gardenia bushes my gramma planted long before I was even a thought in anybody's head.

"On to home. She ain't up to looking for treasure today." Bobby crossed his arms over his tanned chest. "She's reading."

I nodded. "Come on in whilst I fix something to eat." I pushed the screen door open, and Bobby slipped inside. "But keep it down. Daddy is in mourning." Saying them words made my heart feel all alone in my chest.

I padded through the house, Bobby following close

enough I felt his hand touch my own. He was warm from being outside.

"Want something to drink? Everybody brought stuff since the funeral."

"They do that, don't they?" Bobby said. "Yeah, I'll take some ice tea. Same thing happened to us when Nanny went. We got so much food my momma had to freeze it. We ate good for a long time."

"So what's Martha reading?" For a moment, I remembered me and Grampa in the living room in front of a fire during the cold months. Him reading from *The Cat in the Hat*. Him telling me the world was a terrific place with books like this for girls like me to read. I wasn't but a baby in that memory. Momma *and* Gramma both sat on the edge of it, smiling, like they waited permission to come in to the remembrance.

"Some Nancy Drew thing. Boringest book ever."

I pulled sandwich makings from the refrigerator, and made two. One for me and one for Daddy, later, once he got hisself up. Then me and Bobby headed off for the lake, me eating as we went.

Bobby rowed and I hunted, peering into the water, the sun shining back into my face like the lake was a mirror. I thought I might go blind.

At long last I flopped into the boat, my brain aching. "Let's rest," I said.

"Sure," Bobby said. He flung the concrete block overboard. It hit the water with a plunk, bubbles rising. Then Bobby went to the bow of the boat and dove like a professional, sending me in a circle, the craft pulling at the rope. I waited for him, watching. I could see him fine, golden-colored under the surface. Ripple-y looking. Stretched out some. When he come up for air, his hair hung in his eyes. He said, "You a swimmer, Libby Lochewood?"

"What Florida Cracker ain't?"

His arms and legs worked to keep him steady in the water. "Come on in then."

So I did. I dived at Bobby, my orange culottes tugging at my hips when I sliced into the lake.

I came up for air just past him.

"This is a good place," he said, nodding. "The whole of this—what you got here. It's real nice."

"My grampa bought it when land in Florida didn't cost hardly a dime." I swam to Bobby. "Him and Gramma got this place before any of their kids was born. Grampa said it wasn't nothing but weeds and snakes and woods back in the olden days."

We were face-to-face. For a moment I could imagine

what the place looked like way back. When it was full of people. Full of love.

"Me and Martha wasn't born here in Florida," Bobby said. Water ran in streams from his hair, traveling down his tanned face to his neck, before joining up with the lake again.

"No?" The lake was fine on my skin. Cool and like silk.

"No. We come down from Tifton, Georgia, when we was almost three. Been here ever since."

In the water, me and Bobby were the same height.

"Yes sir. Been right here in Lake Mary since."

"Me, too," I said. "But I was born in Sanford." I looked off across the lake and past the trees like I could see the old red brick hospital if I stared hard enough.

"You got water on your lips," Bobby said.

A wind stirred up some, and the boat pulled against the anchor. I could hear the *lap, lap, lap* of waves smacking the wooden side.

"I got water all over," I said. I waved my arms, and Bobby reached out and took ahold of my hand.

"What you thinking of doing?" I waited for an answer. It took a minute for us to find a way to keep treading water with our hands together.

He shrugged. "Nothing."

Our feet worked the water. "I ain't but twelve," I said.

"Me too," he said.

"Almost thirteen."

He nodded. "You know what? This reminds me of a girl what got ate up by a alligator. In water just like this."

"You read about that?" I said.

"In the paper."

"I see."

"She was out in the St John's River with her boy-friend. People on shore heard her scream. Once. Found her right foot. That's all that was left."

"What about her boyfriend?" I glanced around, a nervous giggle crawling up the back of my throat.

"He got a scratch on his belly."

That didn't seem fair. He got a scratch and all they found was her right foot?

"You got gators out here?"

I shrugged. "Maybe." Though truth be told I had never seen hide nor hair of one.

We were quiet then, holding hands in the water, until I said, "Time to get back to work."

Chapter Six

When Grampa came for a visit that night, I near slept through it. He had to call me three times. His voice worked its way into my dream where a perch with pink lips said my name over and over.

"Saw you swimming," Grampa said, when I sat up. "Saw you in the lake."

My face burned. "I, uh . . ." Did he see Bobby holding my hand?

Grampa didn't let me finish. "Life is for experience, Libby. It's for making choices. Life is for living."

He sat quiet for a long moment. Then he scooted up near me. I leaned my head on his shoulder, the buzz of him sounding in my ear. I felt bubbly with happiness that he was here. Even if he *had* seen me with Bobby.

"What's the matter?" I said. "You lonely on the other side?"

"Lonely? Heavens, no. I got meetings to go to, people to visit. All them reunions. Lessons to learn, what I didn't get done when I was with you. I got lots to do over there. No time for loneliness."

"Then what is it?" I said. "You seem sad."

Grampa let out a sigh what sounded like it come from the bottom of his shiny feet. "I was wondering if you found what I left yet?"

I shook my head. "I'm not real sure what I'm looking for."

"I can't tell you," Grampa said. "You have to find it on your own."

"Could you give me a hint?"

Grampa patted my hand, sparks flying, then put it to his lips. I felt a sizzle on my skin there, and I wondered if it would leave a mark.

"How about this?" he said, like he was thinking. He leaned back a little. "How about the hint is 'You'll know it when you see it'?"

I squished my eyebrows together. "That ain't much of anything. I was looking for something a little more . . . I don't know . . . solid. Then I might be able to find whatever it is *easier*."

Grampa stretched his arms way over his head. Out of the tips of his fingers came light like electricity. It reached to the ceiling, making the knotty pine look yellower than the sun. "I got a message for you, Libby."

I straightened up real quick. "Who from?"

"Gramma says hello."

"She does?" I couldn't help smiling. I could almost see her working in her flower garden, the memory came to me that quick.

"And your momma."

"Momma?" Something warm moved in my heart.

"She says she loves you."

I sat still and quiet. "Then why ain't she coming to visit?"

"Well," Grampa said, slapping at his knees. Sparks shot through the wall, and I wondered if they dropped into the bathtub in the next room. "I done said too much already."

"Grampa." He was leaving, and I didn't want him to. I didn't like it that he was gone during the day. It was lonely here, even with Daddy, who looked the other way sometimes when he saw me. And I had no idea how long any of this visiting would last. Maybe one night I would go to sleep and Grampa would not stop in. The thought give me the cry-babies. And now there was Momma. It made me anxious. I hadn't seen her in so long. Couldn't even remember her. Nothing. Not her smell. Not the way her hair fell around her shoulders. Not her hands on my face. Why, I had just the *hope* of her in my head.

"I'm gonna check on your daddy, Libby," he said. "Part of my job for now is to help look out for them what's left behind."

"But you'll be back?" Tears popped into my eyes. Hadn't even been expecting them.

"Of course," he said. "For now." Then he looked good and hard at me. Musta seen the tears, I guess, though I tipped my head down. "I'm here for you, Libby, long as I can be. You just keep your eyes peeled while you're working." Grampa pulled me tight in a hug.

"I can do that," I said.

Then he was gone from my room, though the glow from his hug stayed, like a warm blanket, until I was sound asleep.

"And God said . . ."

Sunday morning found Daddy and me sitting in the Lake Mary Church of Christ meetinghouse. The place smelled of old shoes and sweat. Wasn't a bit of fresh air. Not blowing in from outside nor manufactured, either.

Someone—a man preacher before Melinda Burls—had painted the windows shut tighter than the neck of a tied balloon. You couldn't open those things for nothing. I tried once when we rolled into church early.

But Preacher Burls used the closed windows as lesson material. She said the heat in the summer wasn't nothing compared to Hell's fire. I'm not so sure about that.

This early morning I was thinking about the lake. *Where* was the treasure? And *what* was it? And *why* was it in the lake?

I thought about Bobby and Martha. What did heathens do on Sunday? Were the two of them sweating, too? Was Bobby waiting on me?

After that I thought a whole bunch about the hand-holding me and Bobby had done. Why? Then again, why not? I spent a hour and a half sitting in a stifling hot room in my body—but in my head . . . Ahhh, my head splashed up a storm in the lake.

I even had moments of thinking about my grandfather. Him sitting right beside me when he was alive, letting me lean against his side, him passing the collection plate and goading Daddy into giving more money than just a old, used-up dollar bill.

The whole memory left me smiling big.

All during the closing song, whilst people sort of sang "The Old Rugged Cross," I saw Preacher Burls eyeing

Daddy. She wore a peach-colored dress that shimmered when she moved. Her pearls hung down, swinging this way and that as she directed the song. Her black hair, braided and hanging long down her back, seemed to glow when the lights from above shined on her.

Daddy didn't seem to notice. He was too busy fanning himself with the *Jesus is my Savior Compliments Bartholomew Funeral Home 1967* cardboard fan with the burial times printed right where you could read them.

There are 245 words in that advertisement. Sit long enough in Preacher Burls's presence and there is plenty you will know about your surroundings by the time the main meeting is over. Like how many words is on the funeral fans, how many weeks in a row a spiderweb will hang in a corner of the chapel (seven), and how many bald guys are here on average (thirty-four).

"She's looking at you," I said to Daddy. It was the third time I said it. Daddy shushed me again. Then he fanned hisself. Put his finger in his collar and tried to loosen the thing by tugging at it.

"She's been watching you this whole meeting. Preaching all them words to *you*."

"What you saying, girl?" Daddy turned to me like this was the first time he heard my voice. Dark circles ringed his eyes. He got up to come to church only, telling me he'd be climbing back in bed for five more days. I was okay with that. But looking at his face, seeing his sadness and his tiredness, worried me. I needed to tease him out of things. If he'd hear me.

"You a sinner, Daddy?"

That got his attention. He looked at me all squint-eyed, like I had slapped him a good one right across the face. "We all sinners, girl," he said, spraying the words through his teeth like he does when he wants me quiet. "Now, hush up and sing."

But I couldn't.

"I think we need to make a break for it," I said. "Get on back home. Like Bonnie and Clyde, only we don't kill nobody or rob any banks."

Preacher Burls raised her thin eyebrows at me for talking during the song, maybe. She flapped her arms harder, the beads swaying and swinging with the beat. I could tell she was gonna make us sing the extra verses she had made up. This would be one long closing song.

I leaned into Daddy. "Let's go."

And, surprise of surprises, he did. Right there in the middle of music, Daddy stood, grabbed my wrist, pushed past the Harmons and Castles, and then beat it down the aisle and out the back door, his feet clomping on the old red carpet like he was hell-bent. People stared. But I bet they wished they were as brave as us. I heard the music speed up double time.

As warm as it was outside, the air felt cooler than the inferno we'd been stuck in.

Daddy dropped my arm and said, "Now what, girl? You got any more plans?"

He sounded weary. I wanted to grab ahold of him, give his hand a big love squeeze. Like me and Grampa used to do when we'd go on walks together. I could see Daddy was glad to be free for a minute though he wouldn't have admitted it. He looked at me with his clear green eyes and a bit of smile crept to his lips.

Things were winding down inside the church house, and I knew it wouldn't be long before Preacher Burls would come on outside.

"I want to hightail it outta here," I said. I pulled on Daddy's arm. "Leave Lake Mary for awhile. Head into Sanford. Or go to Daytona. I don't know." Maybe a drive would make him feel better. It had been a good long time since the two of us had done anything together. Why I couldn't even remember the last time it had been just me and him. Mostly it had been me and Grampa.

Daddy nodded. I wished I had the nerve to take his hand in my own. Feel how hard-skinned it was from working for Grampa all his life. He nodded again and headed to our old truck, taking big steps that I had to match two red-Keds steps to keep up.

"Hurry," he said. "Let's git."

We were pulling away when Preacher Burls came to stand out on the steps of the church, her shiny peach dress rippling in the light breeze that blew in from the East.

We didn't stop at home.

"She'll be waiting," Daddy said. "And I need me a breather right now. She's been coming around since your momma died all those years ago."

"Almost nine," I said.

"What?"

"Momma's been gone almost nine years."

Daddy give a little nod.

"Do you miss her?" I'm not sure where the question came from though it seemed to have gotten stirred up from Grampa's visit, like silt in still water.

"Don't have a chance. She's around every week."

"You know I mean Momma."

Daddy eyeballed me.

"Always," he said, his jaw tight. "Miss her in the morning when I get up and at night when I go to bed." He tapped at the steering wheel with his thin gold wedding band. "She is always in the back of my head, sitting there in my memory."

I nodded. I wouldn't a minded having Momma sit in my brain for a little while. At least, I didn't think I would.

"We'll get us some breakfast and we'll talk. We ain't talked in a long time."

"Sounds good," I said. A moth the size of a cat moved in my stomach. Talking with Daddy.

It *seemed* a long time since the two of us had chatted. Before Grampa passed on, Daddy just was. There but not there, if that makes sense. Why, Daddy was as on the outside of my memories as Momma, and she was dead.

We drove all the way to Orlando where Mr. Walt Disney planned to build another park that promised rides and fun all the livelong day. We stopped in at a Big Boy restaurant, and I ate till I thought I might pop. Daddy got me a creamy strawberry milkshake. And did we ever talk.

Really it was Daddy what done the chatting. I grunted when necessary to say I knew what he meant. I was just happy to be away. Happy to be far from the worry that sat on our house like a fat frog near the water's edge. Happy to be sitting with my father. It felt new.

Our waitress, a young girl with curly hair, winked at Daddy as she served him. I don't think he even noticed. He run his mouth the whole hour drive out and back and all during breakfast. Talked about my momma and how he met her (at the roller-skating rink over in Sanford), Gramma and how she died (struck by lightning down at the lake), and how he loved the grove (it was his whole life).

Not me. The grove.

All my happiness sunk away. The newness was gone.

It was on the way home he turned to how we were the Death Family.

Death Family.

There I was, thinking of Momma a little and of Grampa a lot, when Daddy started in. Washed me over like a cold bath, his words did. Shook me up something good. I'd never heard this before. All the other stories—sure—I knew them by heart. But this one was new.

"What do you mean by that? What do you mean 'Death Family'?" I said. My fingertips felt tappy-nervous. I switched off the radio where we'd been listening to WLOF-Channel-95-Watching-Over-You in the background.

I had to hear Daddy better.

"Look at our history, girl." Daddy picked the skin on his thumb till it bled, then he sucked up the blood. He didn't wait for me to answer. Instead, he talked around his finger, one hand hanging limp over the steering wheel.

"My wife dead and you not even four."

I nodded. Momma had slipped during a shower. No one knew she was bleeding in her brain till it was too late.

"My three brothers killed when I was eight." Daddy stared straight at the road. "And I very nearly joined them in their watery grave. Which woulda meant no you."

I nodded again, remembering this story. How Daddy's oldest brother, just fifteen, drove his two other brothers, and two boys from town, off a bridge and into the St. John's River. All of them dead on impact. If Grampa hadn't said, "No, you can't go, Earl," Daddy woulda been in that car.

"Now my own father."

Daddy's face went all limp, like the muscles got tired of doing their work and quit.

"We're the Death Family," he said, his voice a thin whisper. "We are the Death Family."

I sat back on the green seat. My legs stuck to the plastic. My heart thumped.

"Daddy," I said after a minute. I knew I shouldn't but I had to. I tried to stop myself, but I couldn't. It was the right thing to do. "You seen Grampa yet?"

Daddy slammed his hand on the steering wheel. "I *hate* it that you keep on with this, girl."

Outside the gray sky darkened until lightning gashed at the clouds. Rain fell quick, big fat splashes, smacking the windshield and the truck's hood with loud splats. A Florida rain.

I looked away. "I was just wondering."

"Stop your wondering," Daddy said. "Your grand-father *and* grandmother used to ask me that very thing about my brothers and then my wife. My *wife*. 'Did you see 'em yet? Did you see 'em? Did they talk to you?' And then *he* was all the time asking me that about my own mother. Gone from me just a day, and him talking at me about seeing her. He never cried once about her going on."

Daddy looked at me, and I thought I saw a scared look in his eyes.

"Of course, I don't see him. Nor them. Not anyone what's passed. And why not?" His voice sunk to almost nothing. "Because your grandfather is dead. The whole lot of them is *dead*."

Then, so soft I almost didn't hear him, he said, "Only the two of us left, girl. Just you and me. We ain't nothing if we ain't a whole family."

We drove on, listening to the rain.

Chapter Seven

Daddy's words got me to thinking.

What did he mean that Gramma had asked him about seeing the family, gone before him? And Grampa, too? Had Momma ever talked to Daddy about these things? Who else in the family had talked to him about this?

All my thoughts did something to me on the inside. Made my stomach feel pickled. Wrinkled up. Too small for that huge breakfast.

The palms of my hands went numb. My tongue felt like it wore a fuzzy sweater. I could hear water in my ears.

Daddy drove fast through the rain, on back to the house, gripping the steering wheel, his thumb pink where he'd chewed it.

Outside the sky was heavy and dark, though it wasn't even 3:30 in the afternoon.

I cracked the window open, and rain spattered on my arm, making the hairs rise to attention, the drops was that cold. And it only the first few days of September. I took in a deep breath and tried to find some courage in me, but there wasn't any. I think I'd left it all back in the restaurant.

It was a good twenty miles before I said anything.

"Daddy?"

He looked at me, *don't-you-push-me* written all over his face. His look was a dare. His eyes like chips off a RC Cola bottle.

"Tell me what you mean. I got a right to know. I *have* to know." My hands shook. But what I said was true. I needed to find out about this thing that seemed to run in the family. Not including him, I mean. This seeing the dead.

He clenched his jaw. I looked out the window, staring at the rain that made everything seem like a streaky gray sheet, then glanced back at him.

"I'm not trying to get you mad." My voice was low as the hum of the tires on the road.

Daddy didn't flinch. So I pushed on. "Tell me about
. . . about Gramma and Grampa asking you those things
about dead . . ." I paused, searching for the right word.
One that would spell peace for my daddy and give me
needed information. Rain kept falling through the window on me. "About dead family members."

But peace wasn't to happen.

Daddy slammed on the brakes.

I felt like I was on the Tilt-O-Whirl, my face up close
to the dash, then me sliding across that seat as the truck
spun sideways on the water-slick road.

I learned something in those moments. Don't slam on
the brakes in a rainstorm when you are flying down a
two-lane highway upwards of seventy-five miles per hour.
It's dangerous.

My hands went out. One jabbed Daddy in the side.
The other tried to make a hole in the windshield. My feet
pedaled like I was on a bike going downhill.

The tires screamed on the road. Daddy wrestled with
the steering wheel. My head felt like a flag flapping on
a stick in a hurricane. And as far as I could tell, Daddy
never took his foot off the brakes, either.

Lucky for us there weren't too many cars on the road,
what with it being the Sabbath and all. If you ask me, it
was a true miracle we didn't wind up in a ditch or in a
telephone pole or up a palm tree. No. Daddy kept us on

the road, though by the time we stopped, we faced the other direction.

Would he holler at me? Thought sure he would. But Daddy didn't. His voice was low. "What I said then is what I say now." He looked at me with hound dog eyes. "I got no Sight. I don't see the dead." Daddy leaned close. "I ain't no weirdo. And nobody else saw nothing either." His voice was unhappy. Not with me, I knew that. *I* had pushed him to this place. But it was clear one thing bothered him, and I knew what it was. "Nobody else saw nothing either. You hear me?"

I heard.

I knew what he meant, and it bothered me good. Stung. He wasn't seeing no one, even if they were there. Even if it was me.

We drove out of the storm.

By the time we got home, the sky was so bright it near blinded you and gave you a headache besides.

I popped out of the truck, jumping to the ground, before we had come to a complete halt, there was that much pressure built up behind me. Then I run. Daddy didn't even call after me neither. Not that I woulda stopped. He couldn't have made me.

I ran so fast I could feel the wet sand hitting up against the backs of my legs.

"Weirdo," I said. "I ain't no weirdo." But the faster I ran, the more I realized seeing a dead grandfather *was* weird. Having people ask you about seeing dead people was weird, too. I didn't want nobody to tell me I was crazy for seeing people what had gone on before.

I made myself stop thinking by running and concentrating on the way my feet hit the ground.

Thunk! Thunk! Thunk!

Toward the lake I went. The wind whistling past my ears. Sweat running down my forehead, down my cheeks, then tears coming, too. My hair flying out behind me, slapping at my back.

But I *was* thinking, without meaning to. Matching the two-tone beat of my steps.

Gram-pa! Gram-pa! Gram-pa!

Weird-o! Weird-o! Weird-o!

I saw three different snakes in my running. Scared them near to death, I bet, considering they got out of my way in a hurry. I came out of the woods, and there was the lake, like an answer to prayer. Grampa's lake. My lake. I stopped and struggled to breathe. I bent over the way I seen racers do on television during the Olympics.

My heart pounded all over—I could feel it everywhere—even in my skin.

But now that I'd stopped moving the tears really fell. I clinched my eyes shut.

"I saw you," I said to Grampa. I wanted him to know that it didn't matter what Daddy said. I knew what I knew. Wasn't no changing it. I believed.

When I caught my breath, I went on into the lake, waded right out into it, leaving my shoes on and all. We were a swimming family. Always had been.

The water soothed me some, the way it filled in on my feet, then climbed up my ankles, then up my calves. The way it was all warm near the shore, getting cooler as I stepped out deeper. I took a deep breath. To my knees, my hips, my waist. A little deeper and I could kick off and swim. So I did. Taking the water easy. Rolling onto my back and staring up at the sky. Floating. The sun off to the side, shining down like a blanket. The water holding me up like a hand. I could sleep right here. Not worry about a thing. Just sleep.

"Libby?"

I sunk. Caught air before I went down, then pushed to the surface. My head breaking through the lake.

"Libby. It's me."

"Grampa?"

He was in the distance. Thin. See-through out here in

the light, but colored like the water—green and blue and gold with clear mixed in. He was a rainbow of lake color.

"It's me, Libby."

I took a couple of strokes toward him, but he stayed away.

"Just keep put," he said.

"Okay then." I waved my hands, kicked and fluttered my feet to keep myself in one place.

"I heard you with your daddy," he said.

A cool breeze swept past, and the water chopped up some. I nodded.

"He never did believe." Grampa shook his head all sad and sorrowful-like.

"He doesn't believe *me*, that's for sure," I said. A lump caught in my throat. It was like a fish wiggled there. "Doesn't listen."

Doesn't see me.

"Never did. This been happening for generations now." It seemed Grampa talked to hisself, his voice was so low.

"What?" I wanted to be closer to him, but I felt tired. My arms and legs ached. I needed to rest. I swam toward him again.

"Stay where you are now, Libby," Grampa said. His voice was as soft as the setting sun. "You still got to get back to shore."

I turned and looked to where the boat sat on its side on the land and where the raft floated. I was a long way off.

"Like I said," Grampa said, "we been seeing our dead forever. And you got the Sight, Libby."

"Daddy said there ain't no Sight." The water tugged at my hair. Splashed in my eyes, making it hard for me to see Grampa. I wiped at my face.

"Some people . . ." Grampa vibrated with his words, and I saw the opposite shore right through him. "Some people *could* see but don't."

"Why?"

"Won't." He shrugged, and it seemed the land behind him lifted and settled with his movement.

"But why?"

"Too pained to see what could heal them."

Daddy was sure nothing dead could come back to call on the living. As sure as the storm heading in toward the lake from the East.

"Get on back home now," Grampa said.

And he was gone.

Chapter Eight

My arms were stones. My shoes too heavy to move. I was too far out. The wind picked up, and waves smacked me in the face.

Grampa's voice in my head said, "Get on back home now," so I started for shore.

Stroke after stroke, I pulled myself through the water, but when I looked to land again, it didn't appear that I had moved even an inch closer.

"This ain't good," I said. I rolled to my back, hoping for more strength that way. Overhead, gray clouds boiled together, moving fast. Lightning snapped, and I thought of my grandmother struck by lightning whilst on this very lake.

I remembered Daddy talking about it. Gave me goose bumps every time I heard the story. How Daddy and Grampa had watched from the shore as Gramma rowed in to land, trying to beat a sudden storm. And how the wind had come up, making the water choppy and the boat hard to control. And then, from a day sky as dark as night, how a bolt of lightning hit her.

The blast knocked both Grampa and Daddy on their backs. When they got to her, paddling to her on the raft, Gramma's hair was still smoking.

"She didn't feel a thing," Daddy said every time he told the story. "She was dead, just like that." He always snapped his fingers. "No pain."

What she was doing on the water no one ever said, though Grampa had mentioned visiting to Daddy, who got mad.

"She weren't visiting no one," Daddy yelled, whilst I sat in the living room playing with a Barbie and Ken. I was a little thing in the memory. "There was no one on the lake but Momma herself. She was looking at the spot I was gonna build my own place. I am telling you, old man, she weren't visiting no one."

My grampa, he had smiled.

Being dead like that—*snap!*—and not feeling a thing

did not give me any comfort on the lake now. I wanted to get out of the water, wanted to get on back home. Even if Daddy didn't pay any attention to me.

Clouds blocked the sun. The wind grew colder. I kicked hard, and my left shoe popped into the air about a foot and landed in the water. It sat upside down on the surface a moment, moving in the waves like a boat, then sank. I reached for it, but missed.

"Wait," I said. I swished my hands around, grabbing for the shoe, but I couldn't catch it.

"Grampa." My voice was a whisper. This couldn't be happening. I remembered how he had given me these Keds. I couldn't let it get away. Couldn't walk around in just the one I still wore.

I caught myself a huge breath of air and dove down. But my sinking shoe was faster than me, and try as I might, I couldn't get close enough to catch it. When I turned to go back to the surface I realized I was out of breath and in big trouble.

My heart throbbed as I rose toward heaven. My lungs burned. My head pounded. *Get on back home now* bounced in my skull.

I didn't mean to try to take in air, didn't mean to breathe in the lake, but I had to. I *had* to.

Water filled my mouth, my throat, and then my lungs. Tearing into me like a knife. Burning into me like fire.

Every struggle for breath filled me with panic. I jerked around, trying to free myself of the lake. I clawed at the water. I thought of Grampa, and of my daddy and how my dying would make *him* feel. Pain worse than drowning came into my heart thinking of him being all alone in the world.

And that's when I saw it, far across the lake. Something like a light in the darkest part of the water, where it came up deep from a spring. Grampa stood there, smiling. He said, "You're okay, Libby, don't fight so."

I wanted to say something, but I couldn't.

"Go on home, Libby," Grampa said, and though he was far away, he lifted my head above the surface.

Hands reached for me.

"I saw you go down," Bobby said. "I saw you go under."

I looked up. He was crying. I couldn't say a word. I was too full of water.

"I didn't think you was gonna make it." Bobby sobbed. "Your daddy told me you was off and I figured here. When I saw you go down and not come up again . . . I rowed fast as I could . . ." He stopped talking. Then he grabbed me under the arms and pulled me into the boat. It tipped with his weight and mine. When my stomach hit the wooden edge, the lake poured out my mouth and nose, like someone had tilted a pitcher full ice tea into a glass.

"You all right, Libby?" Bobby knelt close to me.

Lightning sizzled in the early evening air.

"Am I dead?" I asked when I could finally take in a breath.

"I don't think so," he said. "Sure thought you was, though." He wiped at his eyes with one hand. Still the tears came. "I've read about dead people. I know the stories. I thought you was a goner sure."

I crawled the rest of the way into the boat, fell onto my back, seeing my one foot, bare of the red Ked. Rain splashed on my face. The air tasted sweet, like nectar from an unopened hibiscus flower.

Air, sweet, air.

But, oh, my shoe was gone.

I rested, almost not breathing, and let Bobby row me to safety.

Bobby walked me the whole way home. Neither one of us spoke. I knew if I did, I'd burst into tears on accounta I had lost my shoe. And nearly my life besides. My throat hurt all the way down and so did my lungs. It felt like I had used a cheese grater on my insides—stingy-like. Raw and puffy. I carried my right Ked close to my chest, like a baby.

By the time we were to my place, the sun had settled itself down and mosquitoes bit.

"Look, Libby," Bobby said when we stood at my screened-in porch. "I don't get it."

Not a light burned in my house. Daddy was probably snoring away already. Not even waiting to tell me good night. The thought made something in my chest hurt. My lungs or my heart, I wasn't quite sure which.

"What do you mean?" I said, testing my voice the first time since Bobby rowed me to shore.

Bobby tipped closer.

"I mean, why ain't you dead, Libby? You was under the water a long time. A *long* time." He nodded when he spoke. "I thought for sure I was gonna have to bring your body home to your daddy. I've done research. I know how long someone can stay underwater. You shouldn't be walking here now."

I didn't know what to say. What *could* I say? I *was* near death. Till my grandfather came along.

So I didn't say anything. Just walked on in the house, making sure the door didn't slam. Waking Daddy and telling him what had happened—I couldn't do it. It would be too much for him to listen to.

Too much to tell.

The last thing I heard was Bobby calling out, "Don't

you go back there without me, Libby. Ya hear me? We're searching together from here on out."

But I knew I could make no promises.

I woke up with a start.

Had Daddy called me?

Was it Grampa? Looking at the clock, I saw I had woken a minute too early. It was 2:34. I glanced around the room. My grandfather was nowhere to be seen.

I lay still, not moving anything at all, only my heart beating blood fast through my body. And listened.

Not a sound to be heard except from outside. The frogs saying they were happy for the rain, I expect.

And then there! There it was again. A wail.

A wail of sadness coming from my daddy's room.

His cry made my hair stand on end. I moved my shoe from my chest where I'd slept with it, threw back the covers, and ran like the wind.

When I got close, I crept toward the door. His room was filled with bluish-green light, and I could see, plain as day, my father kneeling beside his bed. He sobbed out loud in his prayer, crying to God to ease his loneliness. I heard him say, "It's just the two of us now. Just me and my girl. A family ain't whole when someone goes missing."

My heart wanted to break in half, Daddy sounded so tore up.

Then I saw Grampa in the corner.

"He won't see me," Grampa said. "My boy won't see me."

And he was crying, too.

Chapter Nine

I backed myself away and went to my room.

My heart felt ragged, wore out.

In all my life I'd only seen my grandfather cry three times—each instance when someone in another family passed on. And now, on the other side of life, where a person shouldn't *have* to weep, he was.

I climbed into bed, pulling my shoe close.

And what about Daddy who couldn't see—not really *see*—on account of his own disbelief? Even with truth standing so close to him?

The whole thing made me feel tired, like a cloth squeezed too hard. Daddy had separated himself from the family without meaning to. This thing that meant so much to him—our family? We could be one, if he would just see. But for some reason, he couldn't.

I lay in bed, holding tight to the Ked, and waited for Grampa. I knew in my heart I wouldn't get a visit tonight. And I wasn't sure I wanted to. His weeping was something awful to witness, those silver tears hitting the floor, sitting there like a puddle of mercury till they evaporated.

The next morning, I got out of bed, aching. Aching for Daddy, for Grampa, and for us as a family. I had to get out and search that dark part of the lake so I could finish this thing. Try to put us back together.

Desire made me move through my morning motions fast.

I *had* to find what Grampa had left. *Had* to bring it back in my hands, walking all the way from the lake holding whatever it was like a new bird. Maybe there was answers waiting for me in the water. And answers, I knew, could bring peace. Especially if whatever it was could be the proof Daddy needed.

I called out for him, my voice cutting through the empty sounds of the house. "Daddy?"

Just the hum of the fridge and the wind chimes as

a breeze blew past the front porch, carrying with it the smell of the September sun.

"You didn't even tell me good-bye," I said when I found the note. It sat on the table under two fat cinnamon rolls. The note said, "Melinda left these for you. I'm in the southwest groves. Will be back by dinner. Daddy." Two squares of grease with lines of brown cinnamon sugar were on the paper. I licked at the sweet butter.

It was strange how Grampa had made up for my daddy. Now the house seemed hollow.

"Good," I said to the kitchen. "Him being gone means I can leave right this second without one iota of trouble."

But I didn't mean it.

I felt lonesome for my daddy. The house was so vacant it made my stomach seem to drop away. Maybe that's why he had gone—early from his mourning bed. Good and bad both. Good that he was up—bad that he felt he had to leave.

Maybe . . . maybe he needed to get away from me.

"Grampa," I said, digging in the fridge for milk, "you aren't the only one he ignores." My own words hurt.

I didn't expect an answer, and I didn't get one. Not one I could hear with my ears, but something popped into my brain anyway. Grampa's voice. These words.

"You got your work cut out for you, Libby. That ol'

boy of mine." I could almost see Grampa shaking his head with the last of the message. A grim smile on his face.

"I know it," I said, though I didn't have a clue what work I had to do.

I sat down at the table, my one bare foot tapping at Daddy's empty chair, and ate breakfast. Halfway through the second cinnamon roll, I thought to check those tears of Grampa's, see if I could still see them.

Quiet, almost not breathing, I went down the hall to Daddy's bedroom. Daddy never said I couldn't go in there, but since Grampa's passing, since all the changes, this room seemed different. Not just a sad man's room. Something else.

I tiptoed in and went to the corner where Grampa had been early this morning. Not a thing to be seen. I dropped to my knees and rubbed my hand where I was pretty sure the tears had been. Nothing.

I didn't get right up. Instead, I stayed there, hoping against hope my daddy would cease being so lonely. And that I would, too. What we needed was something to heal us. The whatever Grampa wanted me to find. At long last, I got to my feet to leave the room.

It was then that I saw Daddy's bed for what it was. A true mess. The beige chenille spread was pulled up to the pillows, but underneath I could see the sheets needed straightening. And that something was hidden there.

Pulling back the spread, I saw them all. There had to be a hundred of them. Pictures. Some small, some big, some so old they were edged in yellow and curled up.

"What have you been doing?" I said, my guts gripping at my backbone from surprise. "Sleeping with all this mess? Oh, Daddy."

My daddy was sleeping with the dead. All of them pictures surrounding the imprint of his body. It was right creepy. Though I wasn't one to talk much. After all, *I'd* slept with one red Ked. To top things off, I'd put that shoe on this morning though it was still damp and smelled of lake and made me walk with a slight limp. Who was I to say anything, knowing what something dear could do for the heart? At least these pictures didn't stink like an old foot.

Still, a bit of sadness seeped into me, like a slow leak.

Daddy had been through all them snapshots. There was all kinds. One of Grampa and Gramma and their boys, Daddy just a baby. One of me and Daddy and Momma down by the lake—I was bare-butt-nekkid. One of a old woman I didn't know. These were all family shots, generations back. There was even a stack of funeral pictures with the dead resting in their caskets.

It took me only a minute to see that Daddy had them arranged in the order people had died. Grampa was on top. I picked up the picture of my grandfather and looked at it close. A tinge of blue outlined his body in the coffin like a halo. I looked closer. He sure seemed dead. Not like he would be up that night and talking to me.

Gramma was next, in her casket. Green outlining seemed drawn around her. A glow.

Then Momma. She had the color red. Daddy's brothers had just a faint line of orange around each of them— the color of a Creamsicle. Daddy's grandmother—yellow.

What *was* this coloring?

I compared funeral pictures to the pictures of the living and saw nothing but the black and white and grays of photography.

So why the glow? I tried to remember Grampa's visits since his dying incident. Yes, there was blue in that. But also brilliant whites and golds. Could there just be something with casket photography?

"What are you doing, girl?"

I screamed and threw the pictures in the air. They fluttered down all around, some landing on the floor, Grampa landing in my lap, the rest on the bed.

"Daddy," I said, clutching the bedspread. "I thought you was off working."

He stood in the door, tired-looking.

"I come back to check on you," he said.

"You never done *that* before." My heart pounded so I could feel it in my wrists.

"Decided to today."

"I'm fine." I gathered the fallen pictures. My face simmered. He'd caught me. Not that I was doing anything wrong, but Daddy had caught me.

"What you doing going through my stuff?" He didn't move except to put one hand in his pocket. A beam of light from the bathroom window filled up the hall behind him. Sun from his windows poured into his room like liquid.

I finished stacking the funeral pictures, patting them to make the edges neat.

"First," I said, not sure what else to say. I didn't want to talk about Grampa's tears, and I didn't want to leave my looking. "First, I was gonna make the bed. Then I saw these." I waved at all the photos.

"So?" Daddy said. He shifted to his other foot and ran a hand through his hair.

I hadn't expected that kind of answer from him. Maybe from Bobby and Martha. Or from me. But my daddy? Why, he sounded like a kid with his "So."

"I, uh." I stood. A few stray pictures fell to the small rug placed next to Daddy's bed. His prayer rug, where he knelt in the nights and mornings to talk to God.

Me and Daddy stared at each other. Him looking real young. Me feeling all soft and sad for him.

A memory hit me.

It was a long time ago, and it was me and Daddy . . . and Momma. Yes, she was there, at the edge of things. I was on her lap. Daddy was home from working with Grampa. He came in the room to us and scooped us both up close, smiling all the time. When was the last time I had seen my daddy smiling good and strong?

That memory was gone fast as it came. Without even thinking about it, I walked over to my father and put my arms around him. He was warm and smelled of oranges and grove soil. I could feel the muscles in his back. I rested my head on his chest and listened to the beating of his heart. My eyes burned. I could feel his loneliness. Could almost touch it. If I had put out my tongue, I mighta tasted that loneliness in the air.

"It's all right now," he said, keeping his arms tight to his sides. "You're gonna be fine, girl." Then with one hand he pat-patted me.

I wanted to say, *But what about* you? *Are* you *gonna be okay? Are you gonna make it?*

'Cause standing there in that room, the sunlight pouring in all around us, the dead close enough to touch, I saw that it *was* just the two of us remaining. I took in how awful it would be for the other if one of us left. How close I had come the day before. I wasn't ready for it yet. Not yet.

And I didn't want my daddy going nowhere, neither.

Even if we didn't talk much. We had to stay close, no matter what gift some of us Lochewoods had. The two of us had to stay together.

"I love you, Daddy," I said.

He thumped my back two more times. Then he said, "I'll get the pictures up if you get your shoe offa my bed."

I glanced over. Right there on Daddy's pillow, my left red Ked, back again.

Chapter Ten

I made sure Daddy was good and gone before I went for the photos again. Made sure his ol' truck had bounced away from the house. Called out to him, "See you right before dinner."

He kept the photos all in a trunk that I found under his bed. Separated into sections by years, it looked like.

"At least you're not trying to hide it," I said to Daddy, who was probably all the way to the main dirt road that led to the packing warehouses.

I dragged the pictures into my room. The trunk lid lifted without a squeak, and the smell of old paper fluttered near.

"This is better sorted than a library," I said, staring down at years and years—generations—of photographic history. Why, everyone I ever knew and everyone I didn't was in this here box. With one finger I touched a label glued to the trunk. *Magillicutty Line* was written in spidery letters. Not Daddy's handwriting, that was for sure.

There was *Lochewood Line, Oliver Line,* and *Tittle Line,* too. All in that same thin handwriting. Looking in this box was like looking into the past.

I felt someone near. Like I wasn't alone. Not Grampa's feeling. Someone else. Who?

I glanced over my shoulder. No one. I looked back at the stack of pictures. The feeling of someone standing near my shoulder bloomed up behind me. Sitting real still, I let the feeling wash over me from the top of my head on down. Warm and soft.

"Libby?"

"Who are you?" My voice came out a whisper.

"Libby?"

"I'm here." I closed my eyes.

"Libby!" This time my name was a screech.

It was Martha's voice, not someone from my past.

"You in there?"

And Bobby.

"Coming," I said.

I dragged the trunk into the front room and went to the door. "Hey," I said through the screen.

"Hey to you. I finished my book," Martha said. Today her hair was pulled into two uneven ponytails. They still looked tangle-y. I had no idea how she got those things up. "Thought I'd come and help search for the gold."

"She wants part of the reward," Bobby said, using his thumb to jab at his sister.

They waited outside the door. Bobby's ragged cut-offs hit his knees. Martha had on the same yellow dress from before, but it looked clean as a whistle. Both of them stood barefoot. I looked past them, searching for someone I might recognize from one of Daddy's pictures. There was no one.

"I'm checking something," I said. "Hoping for clues. Come help me."

They followed me into the living room.

"I am good at figuring out clues," Martha said. "I have figured out all the Bobbsey Twins books, and Nancy Drew, and the Hardy Boys, too. Most time before I finish them."

"Then maybe you can help," I said. I thumbed through the stack of pictures marked *The Deceased* till I found the ones I'd held earlier. Lots of the dead wore a halo.

I held out the ones of Momma and Gramma and Grampa in their caskets. "Lookit."

Bobby took the pictures. "This is your grandfather," he said.

"Yuck. All these people are dead," Martha said.

"Yes, I know," I said. "But lookit real hard at them three photographs. What do you see?"

Martha took one. "A stiff." She shivered. "Why do you take a picture of the deceased, Libby?"

"I didn't. Somebody else did. I guess it's tradition." I tapped the photo. The color vibrated and settled. "What else do you see?"

"This your momma?" Bobby held her picture in the palm of his hand, like he loved it.

I nodded. "She passed on when I was little. Fell and hit her head." No need for them to know she was in the shower. There's something about being nekkid that is too much information to give to someone not related.

Martha took in a deep breath. "I don't see nothing in this 'cepting they are all goners." Again she shivered.

"I can see you look a lot like your momma," Bobby said after a minute of staring at the three pictures. "And she seems to have been a right nice woman."

"Can you see that color?" I traced the picture with a finger, causing the light to shimmer.

"What color?" Martha said. "There ain't nothing there."

Bobby stared at Momma.

"I see where you get your smile," he said to me.

"She ain't smiling," Martha said. "You are a nut. You are seeing things, Bobby. The woman in that picture is deader than a doornail. Not meaning any offense, Libby."

"Not at all," I said and peered over Bobby's shoulder at the photographs he now held like cards, all splayed out.

"Let me have them back," I took the photos and glanced at Momma. She *was* smiling. I hugged the picture to my heart and looked again. Yep, the smile was still there.

Well, well, well.

I saw it in the far corner of the lake. That light. Past Grampa when he told me to go on home and I'd gotten delayed by my own drowning.

"Let's head out thataway," I said when Bobby, Martha, and me ended up at the shore. I pointed far across the lake, where the water looked like ink and trees grew in close.

"Think there are snakes out there?" Martha said. She already sat in the boat though it was pulled up onto dry ground. Bobby pushed the small craft, made heavier with Martha in it, out of the sand whilst I looked over the water and talked to Grampa with my mind.

You gotta show me what it is. I can't do it alone. You gotta be with me now like you was every step of my life.

There was no answer. Only Bobby's grunting out, "Martha, there are snakes all over this state."

"But are there any over *there*?"

I stepped into the ankle-deep water with Bobby, and we pushed Martha out further. The boat burst free from the earth and slipped from our hands.

The air felt like a hot, wet blanket. Clouds billowed in the East, bringing a storm our way.

"We don't have much time," I said, and stepped into the boat. I grabbed an oar and nodded toward the sky.

"I can do that," Bobby said. "I can row."

"It's a long way," I said. "We'll share the work."

The sun struck at the water and our faces and backs. It heated the air in the small boat. The coming storm would be a relief.

"How sweet, you two lovebirds," Martha said, and she tugged at a ponytail, making the rubber band slide closer to her scalp. "Working together like that."

"You shut up," Bobby said. Then he smiled at me.

I looked at my hands on my oar and bit into the water with it, so I didn't have to show Bobby my face that I was sure was pink from embarrassment and pleasure. "Let's get this show on the road," I said.

Chapter Eleven

It was a long way across the lake. And the whole time I worried.

Sure Daddy said me seeing things meant I was a weirdo, but, well, maybe Bobby and Martha . . . they might get it. They might understand what I was talking about, but the thought of telling them made my heart thrum like a hummingbird had been set loose inside of my ribs.

Martha kept the post of peering into the water. She kept her mouth going with "Saw a fish. Saw another fish. Ain't no gold out here yet. There's nothing. Just the bottom of the pond. By now Nancy Drew woulda found the loot."

I could tell by the way Bobby ground his teeth that he was aggravated with his sister.

"Cain't you keep your mouth shut?" he said after a while.

"I'm doing my duty," Martha said. "Earning my share."

"I'm not so sure we're gonna be finding that much out here," I said.

"One gold coin is a haul to me," Martha said. She went back to her reporting. "Nothing in my sight but water. There's a stick. Nothing but . . ."

Bobby ground his teeth.

"I got something to say." My voice surprised me. I hadn't realized I was gonna open my mouth yet.

"All right then," Bobby said. He let the oars rest in his hands.

"Come out with it," Martha said, peering into the water still. "I got reporting to do."

I cleared my throat. "You know my grampa passed on."

Overhead the storm clouds puffed up like a fire burned somewhere.

Bobby give a nod. Martha grunted yes.

"That night, after he was buried, he come for a visit. He come to see me."

I squinted as though the sun was bright overhead though the sky had turned dark.

In slow motion, Martha looked up from the water. "Who come to visit you?" she said. Her voice sounded a lot like Daddy's when he's frustrated with the dead talk.

"My, um, my grampa." I hesitated. Took in a breath. "He visited me. It was him who told me there was something hid out here."

They both looked at me like the top of my head was gone.

Maybe this wasn't such a good idea after all. The sun got lost behind a black cloud.

"You saw your dead granddaddy?" Martha said.

Bobby said nothing.

And then we were to the opposite shore. And not a moment too soon. The storm broke wide open.

"Are you crazy?" Martha said. Wind pushed at her hair. "What do you mean, you seen your dead grampa? That's sick."

Lightning blinded me like the flashbulb on Daddy's camera. Thunder banged like a giant drum hit right by my ear.

"I did," I said. I stood in the boat wobbling with the waves that smacked the side. Martha stood too.

"Liar," she said to my face.

Lightning crackled.

Gramma! I thought.

"Get off the water," I said. "Get off quick."

Martha looked at me wide-eyed and without a question leaped into the lake and headed toward the trees.

Snap went lighting. Clap went thunder. Sheets of rain fell, soaking me to the skin in moments. Things was so loud, I couldn't even hear my own heart. Just felt it, pounding like it wanted to leave this storm without me.

The hair stood up on my arms. "Get out of the boat," I hollered at Bobby. I leaped after Martha, sinking into soft sand to my ankles, the water high as my knees. Rain splashed around me, popping the lake up like bullets. I fell, went all the way under. Someone tugged on my arm. Martha pulled me up. Her eyes were as big around as Parson Browns, fear stretching the skin over the bones in her face.

Bobby plunked into the water, too. Then we all rushed to shore, jerking the boat up behind us. The trees shadowed the land like thick eyelashes.

"Cain't stay under a tree," Bobby said.

And so we ran, leaving the boat to rest.

I had never been to this part of my grampa's—I mean mine and daddy's—property. It's not that I wasn't allowed. Just never had reason before. But here we were, the wind whipping through the trees, slinging Spanish moss like the weather had hands.

"Where do we go?" Martha said, plowing ahead, bent over at the waist. Her yellow dress was so drenched and clingy I could see the bones in her back. Her hair hung in strands like an unwoven rope. Her arms paddled at the air moving her along.

Where *do* we go? I thought, panicked. Into the empty field that spread out in front of us? Or stay in the trees?

Bobby stopped dead-still though the rain hit like slaps. "Now what?" he said.

The sky was green. I opened my mouth in a scream but heard nothing but the explosion of thunder.

"I don't know," I said, yelling in his ear. "Just lay flat." And down I went into the mushy ground, my face pressed into the earth. The wet grass made me itch, and all I could smell was dirt.

Lightning lit up everything around us again and right then I knew I had made a mistake.

Yes, I had.

Martha wasn't supposed to be here.

This search was something I could do only with Bobby.

Martha bawled. Tears ran down her face, mixing in with rainwater and the lake.

"I ain't coming back again," Martha said, screaming when lightning bit at the air around us.

"You don't have to," I said. But I wasn't sure she

even heard me, what with the blast of thunder that followed.

"He's good choice, ol' Bobby," Grampa said that night. "He believes in you."

"I hope so," I said. "'Cause Martha sure don't." I snuggled in close to Grampa. He smelled of roses, and tonight he looked even younger than before. He had hardly any wrinkles. His hair seemed blonder, though it was hard to tell with all the blue and white and golden light. If he kept this up, I'd appear older than him soon.

"Don't forget this is different for people," Grampa said. "Look at your daddy. This here gift runs in his own family and he don't get it. He's scared."

Grampa had a point with that one. Best I should keep my mouth closed with Martha. Between her and Daddy, it was him I wanted to convince, not her. If I had to use my energy for something, it would be for my father.

We sat quiet, me sitting close to my grandfather. I held my breath and thought how lucky I was. Poor ol' Bobby. He couldn't see his nana. But me, I was with my most favorite person in the world. And him gone on to the other side, too.

"What'd ya think of the pictures?" Grampa said.

I let out a laugh. "You mean all those colors?"

Grampa smiled, and the room lit right up. "It's a re-minder of us. So you don't forget."

A reminder. I sucked in a deep breath of air and watched the light around Grampa move with my breath-ing. Oh, I loved him!

"You doing okay?" I wrapped my arms around his waist and leaned my face against him. The same elec-trical buzz I felt during the lightning storm came from my grandfather now, brushing my cheek, fluttering like butterfly wings near my eye. But this time I wasn't one bit afraid.

"Oh, yes," Grampa said. "I am doing real good. Keeping up the work of the dead. Waiting on you to see what will happen."

I looked at Grampa, and he smiled down at me, sparks flying like a sparkler going on the Fourth of July. Light popped from him and landed with a sizzle on my arm.

"Am I getting closer?"

He nodded.

"And do you think Bobby will be a help?"

Again he nodded. Light showered onto the bed, where the spots glowed and then went out like a lightning bug blinks off. "He should be able to."

"Because he believes?" I said.

"Because he cares."

He cares? Okay then.

We sat quiet a good long time.

"You know, Grampa," I said, "it won't be long."

"Till what?" Grampa said.

"Till Daddy believes. In you. You know, in you being here."

Grampa looked toward the wall like he could see his son lying in the bed in the next room. "I hope you're right, Libby. It's been years I worked with him, and he refused me. We need him to be complete, you know. A family ain't whole if someone is missing." Grampa let out a sigh that sent the smell of spearmint out to me. It was cool, like lake water is when you swim over a spring. "We got to get things cleared up for you here."

"We will," I said. But I wasn't as sure as I sounded.

Next morning I was awake before the sun even had a chance to peek over the oak trees. Daddy, I could hear, moved around in his room.

I didn't have a plan. Didn't know what to do at all. So I sat on the edge of my bed and sucked in air till it felt like my lungs might pop. Then I got up, got dressed, and went to Daddy's door. After a second, I said, "You in there, Daddy?" though I knew he was.

"I am, girl," he said. He opened the door to me. He wore Levi's and a old blue paint shirt.

"What are your plans?" My heart slowed.

Daddy gave me the old "What do you mean?" eyeball. "I have to go to work. Same as every day."

We stared at each other, Daddy a good head-and-a-half taller than me.

"At the grove?"

"Where else?

Again we stood quiet.

"Ain't you going to ask me what I'm off to do?" I crossed my arms and waited, hoping my heart's beat didn't show through my striped shirt.

Daddy let out a breath that smelled like sour morning and old coffee. Not a thing like spearmint.

He crossed his arms and said, "Girl, what are *your* plans for the morning?" A weak smile tried to find a home on Daddy's lips.

"Why, thank you for asking," I said. "I'm off to find my family what's gone on before."

The smile slid from Daddy's face. It was almost like I could see it splat on the floor.

Time to leave. Just get his attention and hightail it outta here. A fine plan. I turned on my heel and marched out the house, not even stopping when I heard my father call me from the front porch.

Bobby came outside and stood on the concrete block step of his trailer house the second time I hollered for him. So did Martha. She looked all bent out of shape, but I saw her hair was brushed up nice and shiny.

She put her hands to her hips.

"I told you yesterday, Libby, we ain't coming back."

"What?" Now the sun had crept up. Thin fingers of light scratched the tops of the trees, promising a hot day. And the regular afternoon summer storm that means Florida.

"You go on home and do your gold search without Bobby and me. You crazy thing—saying you saw your dead grampa."

Martha's words were like a slap on the mouth. I couldn't think of a thing to say back to her.

"I done told our momma, and she said Bobby cain't work on that lake again. She said only a fool would be looking for gold bullion out there. And what if we got us a stomach cramp and drowned?"

Bobby scratched at his arm. He wouldn't look at me. Just down at his feet.

I didn't care so much if Martha stayed behind, but I needed Bobby.

"I never said it was gold we was looking for, Martha,"

I said. "I never said it was bullion. I told you I was searching for treasure." Pain climbed up behind the back of my
nose. Lucky for me I was too far away for either of them
to see my eyes get wet so fast. "And anyway, you're the
ones who volunteered."

"We are un-volunteering. It's dangerous out there. All
those storms. All that lightning. And snakes." She pointed
at me. "Not to mention you are a fool."

"Okay then," I said. I turned away, hoping to hear
Bobby call me back. But all that came was Martha's
voice.

"We don't expect no payment if you do find anything.
Even though we did work all them hours."

I raised my hand in answer and hurried away.

Bobby never said a thing.

Heading home, embarrassment cooked my cheeks. I
hadn't said anything about gold. That had been Martha
all along. I had never asked them for their help. Not
Martha. Not Bobby.

It was a lonely, hot walk back to the lake.

First thing I did was kick off my red Keds—so I
didn't lose one again—and slip into the water to swim.
I scanned the lake, looking for Grampa. But I didn't see

him. I floated on my back, cried for a few minutes, then determined I would be fine without Bobby.

Talking about Grampa? That had been dumb.

Talking about the dead? Why should *they* believe when Daddy wouldn't?

Yes, that was my mistake. I had done it all wrong.

"It wasn't like I needed him along," I said to the sky.

The words got stuck in my throat. I *did* need him. With Grampa gone, things was too quiet at home. Daddy off to bed early in the evenings and then up and off to work even earlier the next morning. Ignoring me. Bobby was good company. He'd seen Momma's smile. I wasn't so alone when he was around.

Anyway, the one time I had gone off by myself, I had near drowned. If Bobby hadn't come up when he did, who knows what would have happened to me. I mighta ended up as fish food. Fish nibbling at my bones. *That* made me shiver.

Water filled my ears. I stared at the heavens, cloudless and blue as the ocean. I waved my hands to keep me steady.

"At least you don't have to tell Martha she can't come along anymore," I said as I backstroked to shore. It was time for work.

I sat in the morning sun awhile, my stomach calling out to me. But maybe I had to do this today without eating. Sacrifice a little. Go without food a few hours. Maybe that would help.

Taking in a deep breath, I pushed out the boat to row to the far side of the lake. That's when I heard him. Then turned to see him.

"Don't go yet, Libby."

Bobby. Calling my name.

Leaping down the sand path. Hair flapping when he jumped. Shirt open as he made his way to the lake.

I swallowed, swallowed. Said, "I thought you weren't allowed to be with a weirdo" when he stood in the water next to me. I tried not to smile, but I coulda kissed that ol' Bobby.

He shrugged. "They don't know I'm here," he said, all out of breath. "And besides, Martha ain't allowed to tell me what to do."

Bobby climbed into the boat.

I squinted at him. "I seen my grampa," I said.

"I believe you, Libby."

We rowed straight away.

Chapter Twelve

Reeds edged this side of the lake, standing tall and thick like a hideout. We were a good hundred yards from them, parked over the spring—where I was sure Grampa was—if he was here at all.

"Don't let us drift over that way," I said, pointing to the brown and green grasses. "It's a nesting place for something ugly."

Bobby nodded and threw the block overboard. It thudded into the water, then sunk, sending bubbles to the surface and pulling the rope tight.

"As good as I can figure," I said, "this is the place."

Bobby peered over the side of the boat. "I cain't see the bottom," he said. "It's dark. Muddy, almost."

"Yeah, it's deep."

He nodded. "Now what?"

I looked at the sky. No rain in sight. At least not yet. "I think we got us a good hour or two to scout around, check out what's down there."

"And still make it home before any thunderstorm what might come."

Both me and Bobby looked around like we was weather experts.

I nodded. Not too far away a bass jumped, catching air and throwing light back at us, showing his rainbow side. The lake lapped at the boat with a *thwip, thwip, thwip*. There was no other sound but us talking. So quiet out here, it was almost reverent. The quiet made me want to keep my voice low.

Bobby stood in the boat and hitched his shorts up some with his thumbs. "How about I go in first? See what I can see." He flipped his hair sideways, but it fell back into his eyes.

I glanced at him. "You worried?"

"Naw, not really." He peeked over the side of the boat, then threw me a look. "Maybe a little."

"No need." Was it the sun making me feel so good? "I'm an excellent swimmer."

Bobby nodded. "It was just last time. Scared me is all."

I looked him right in the eye. "That won't happen again."

And it wouldn't. I couldn't leave Daddy alone. Not yet. It would be too much. He had to know for himself about our family. It was my job to teach him, and I had to be alive to do it.

"So me first then," Bobby said. Without another word, he dove into the water, sending the boat in a circle as it strained against the anchor.

I watched. I could see Bobby fine, the way he pushed against the lake. He didn't go too deep, but worked this way and that until he ran out of breath and surfaced.

"See anything?" I said, though I was sure he wouldn't.

Water fell like a sheet down his face. He ran his hand through his hair, making it stand on end.

"Only light."

My heart felt like it slowed then jumped to beat double time. "What?"

"I'm not real sure. Some kind of light. Like something offa *Star Trek*. You know when they tell Scottie to beam them aboard the ship?"

I nodded. I knew that show. Daddy watched it every Friday night, making fun of the people traveling through space and time, but still staring at the screen like nothing was more important than that cool television program.

"It's glittery like that. Let me check again." Bobby sucked in air a few times then dove. His final kick splashed droplets the size of dimes into the boat. They evaporated in a moment.

"Now what is it?" I said under my breath to Bobby, Jell-O-y-looking beneath the surface. Had we found the hiding place after all? And what was hidden? I knew it wasn't gold bullion, but something far more important than that. Something family? Hope the size of a grand-pappy catfish came with that thought.

Bobby swam up to the side of the boat. He grabbed it like he was going to pull himself in but instead spoke up to me. "You gotta see this, Libby." His voice was a whisper.

"What?"

I didn't wait for an answer, just jumped, cannon-ball-style, into the cool lake. I popped up next to Bobby. "Tell me." Excitement ran all through me. I felt it bub-bling in my ankles. If I had been standing, I wasn't so sure they woulda held my weight.

"It's more clear if you're in the shadow of the boat."

"Okay."

"You don't have to go that deep."

I nodded. Sucked in the air to dive.

"Now wait, Libby." Bobby grabbed my arm.

"What?" I shivered. I *had* to see what Bobby saw. I had to bring whatever it was back to Daddy and make him believe. I had to make things right for Grampa. For Daddy. For us all.

"You gotta be careful."

"I will," I said. I tried to wiggle free of Bobby's hand, but he held me tight.

"Promise me you'll be careful, Libby."

We floated in the water to our necks, our feet moving like dancers'.

"Promise?"

"I will," I said.

"No matter what you see?"

"No matter what I see."

Bobby took my hand, led me to the other side of the boat, and then we went under.

The light reminded me of family. I can't say why.

And there, in the distance, like someone had built a fire underwater, was a shimmer. A glow. A glimmer.

Bobby pointed, and I saw the book. Pages waving all soft-like. Fluttering like a wind blew. Like it was suspended in pudding.

It was real and I had it in my hands in no time. Saw words I could almost read. Names, it seemed. But I couldn't make any sense of it. Like when you dream and you're lost and you can't find your way, no matter what.

I pushed to the surface, Bobby close behind. When my face met air, I couldn't breathe. Not for a moment anyway. I don't even know if I woulda heard myself if the water hadn't sent the sound back to my ears. "What did you see?" I touched my throat.

"That book."

I nodded, lifting it out of the lake. The book was heavy with water. "What else?"

"Just light. Wiggly light."

Neither one of us said a word.

And then Bobby. "What is it?"

"I don't know."

"I tried to swim closer, Grampa, but I couldn't ever git there. It was like everything moved away from me. Couldn't catch a deep enough breath."

My grandfather crossed his knees and nodded, lighting up the room with his movements.

"Was it 'cause Bobby was there?"

"Bobby?" Grampa let out a laugh that echoed around the room. For a moment it was like we stood in full sun. "No, Libby. Let me tell you something." He leaned near, and I reached out for his hand.

Boy, did I ever want Daddy to feel this. To know that

his daddy was okay. To not have to feel awful loneliness anymore. That would be something wonderful to share.

"Before I married your grandmother, I knew she belonged. She fit in. She was ready to see, too."

"See?"

Grampa waved his hands at himself like he was the answer.

Realization tapped at my brain. "What? You mean it's not just our family?"

"'Course not. You think it's just *us* that's not meant to be so wore out with sadness?"

I shrugged. "Preacher Burls says pain is part of life."

"It is. But there's a plan for us all—the whole world. We all have gifts. Most of them different. Some run down lines from one generation to the next. It has to do with our beliefs."

"And Gramma believed?" I settled into Grampa, knowing.

"Right. She wanted to see, so she believed. Believing eases pain some."

Grampa moved like he was restless. He stood, cracked his knuckles. Walked for the wall. "Gotta check on that boy of mine," he said. "Peek in on him."

"Wait," I said, "I got something to show you." I padded over to the dresser where I'd wrapped the book in two towels. Brought it over. Unwrapped it like a present.

It was a ledger. Brown leather. Damp to the touch.

"Well, lookit here," Grampa said. He stretched out his hand, and light reached out with him, leaping to the wall.

"You kept all your notes about money in these," I said, sitting close. "There's a whole bunch in your desk. Daddy goes through 'em every once in awhile."

Grampa nodded. Lit the room with sparks. "This here book, though, it's where I kept other notes. *Family* notes." He touched the cover. Ran a finger down the ridged edge of pages.

"I wondered if there were names," I said, nodding, smiling.

"Did you?"

"Yes, sir. I had that feeling."

Grampa opened the book like it wasn't wet at all. Turned the pages easy as pie.

"Tell me, Grampa." I could see clear there wasn't one word that could be read. Everything was smeared. Gone like fish had eaten the words from the paper.

"Events," he said after a long moment. "Family events."

I looked into his face. Grampa seemed young as Daddy. "You mean about the Sight?"

"That's what I mean, Libby."

I almost couldn't ask the next question. "What was it doing in the water, Grampa?"

He put his arm around me, and a buzz of electricity

ran through my shoulders. "That's for you to find out," he said.

"Was it Daddy?"

Grampa didn't answer.

"Is this what you left me in the lake? Did I find it?"

"You almost got it solved." Grampa sighed.

I jumped up to hug him.

"What's this, Libby?" he said, wrapping his arms around me. I could hear the smile in his voice.

"Some belief from over on this side of the line. For you." Even with the answers seeming close, even with the book and the almost-names, I wasn't sure I could do it. I still felt so helpless. And maybe he did, too. But I didn't want my grampa to know I was worried. No sirree.

Grampa kissed the top of my head. Then off he went through the wall.

I stood still a minute, staring at where he had gone to see Daddy. Then I settled myself into bed, warmth patting at my worry.

Closed my eyes. Moved toward sleep.

"I didn't save you, Libby girl." The words seemed to be a part of a near-dream—one that still might come. "You wouldn't have gone down."

Chapter Thirteen

I *didn't save you, Libby girl. You wouldn't have gone down.* Those was the first words that come to my mind when I opened my eyes and stared at the ceiling the next morning.

What in the world did *that* mean? That I was a swimmer? A pearl diver who could hold her breath long as necessary?

"I believe you, Grampa," I said. My room was bright with daylight. I swallowed a few breaths of air and then, watching my little clock, timed myself.

Just over a minute.

"Makes my head pound," I said. "Maybe sitting up will be easier."

It wasn't.

I *did* need to breathe. Breathing was part of me. Air and my body worked together real good.

I got out of bed, flipping the covers around some so it would look like I had straightened things up. Then I went into the kitchen, ledger behind my back, wondering at Grampa's words. Had I dreamed them? Maybe they weren't part of his visit. But they sure felt real.

Daddy sat at the table, reading the newspaper. Breakfast was spread out all over. Pancakes and bacon, hot coffee steaming in a flowered mug, fried apples, and one glass of fresh-squeezed orange juice.

"Hey, girl," Daddy said. He folded the paper and put it down, looking a little green around the gills—probably because he had to talk to me.

His gaze slowed my words.

"Hey," I said. "We expecting company?"

"No," Daddy said, shaking his head. "Thought I'd do something nice for ya. Seeing how this has been a hard time for both of us. And seeing how school is getting ready to start."

I walked in slow motion to the table. Something didn't seem quite right. Daddy making breakfast? That had been Grampa's job—or mine. To make matters worse, his words about school felt as heavy as an anchor to me.

I slipped the book under my chair, then sat at the table. Tucked a napkin in my old white T-shirt and started in on the pancakes. They were full of pecans. "These are real good."

"Melinda Burls's recipe," Daddy said, nodding. He cleared his throat. Why didn't he have a plate in front of him?

"You ain't eating?" I said.

"I did earlier. Thought you and me could have us a little chat."

Uh-oh.

"Okay." I tried to make myself at ease, but I couldn't quite. Grampa's book seemed large as the room. I kept eating.

Again Daddy cleared his throat. He shuffled his feet some. Clasped his hands like he was getting ready to pray. Then he leaned toward me from across the table. Stared at his fingers. They were stained from working in the orange groves.

The fridge kicked on with a hum.

"You mentioned something yesterday I think we should talk about."

Thump-thump went my heart. Clink went my teeth against the fork. I looked at Daddy only a little bit. I could do his almost-stare, too. Under my chair, the ledger grew bigger and bigger.

"You said," he leaned even closer, "you were going to find our relatives what had gone on."

I stopped mid-chew. There was a fist in my gizzard. "So *that's* what this is about? All this fancy breakfast? Not just to talk to me for me, huh?"

"We need to discuss things, girl," Daddy said. I could hear he meant business. "What were you talking about?"

Still holding my fork, I gave him the strongest look I could, though I felt nervous as a new tadpole around a flock of egrets. Would my voice hold out, or give up and make me sound like a chicken?

"Daddy," I said, "I am searching out the dead."

It sounded okay. Natural.

"The dead." He gasped in the words, then let out a big ol' breath. His eyes narrowed so that it seemed like Daddy stared at me down his nose.

"So," he said. "Before he passed on, my pop was talking to you, huh? Telling you that crap. Filling your brain with Lochewood nonsense, though I told him not to."

The phone rang, but Daddy didn't move to answer it. So neither did I. No one ever calls me anyway.

"He talked to me plenty, Daddy," I said. "Grampa was my very best friend in the world."

Daddy looked away fast. Like there was something interesting on the far wall.

"That's not what I mean. I mean, he talked to you about the dead in our family. He told you he saw them all the time."

"No, he didn't," I said. "Not before he died. He never said a word about it."

Daddy slammed his hand on the table, and my orange juice rippled, splashing onto the tablecloth. "I told him to keep his mouth shut. Not to mention them. To keep this quiet."

"What do you mean *them*?"

He hesitated, wriggled, like he was uncomfortable, like a fish pulled from the water.

"Pop talked about the dead. Told you about seeing Mama. My brothers. Emily."

I didn't answer.

Daddy's whole face got all squinty. "Lookit here, girl." He pointed at me. "He didn't see no one. Not really. It was the dreams of a old, desperate man."

We were quiet, staring at each other over the breakfast table. A fight without words.

"Daddy," I said, after we had listened to the kitchen clock tick off the minutes. My voice was whisper-thin. "Daddy. What if what he saw *was* real?" I reached out to my father. "What if I told you *I've* seen Grampa?"

He watched my hand then said, "The dead are dead, girl." His voice was sad and heavy, like he *wished* he could believe, if only for a moment.

"Not always. Not with us."

Daddy kept talking, like he hadn't heard me. "I had this dream once," he said. His voice got all quiet. "About your momma. Right after she was gone."

I held my breath. Did not blink. Outside a breeze blew through the wind chimes, making them sing.

"She come to my room in light like a rainbow late one evening . . ." Daddy stopped his talking. Looked like he was feeling out the memory. He almost smiled. "I loved her more'n my own life. I said, 'You can't be here, Emily. This ain't possible.' And the dream faded."

I swallowed.

"I never had it again."

"Why, Daddy," I said, whispering. "That wasn't a dream. You saw her. You saw Momma." The warm feeling from a couple of days before came back to settle around my shoulders like a shawl.

I pulled out the ledger. Set it near his coffee cup.

"What is that?"

Now *I* didn't say anything.

"Where'd it come from?"

Daddy's face was like a cooked lobster. His hand shook

as he reached for the book. It left a damp place on the tabletop.

"Where?"

I cleared my throat. Wrestled inside for strength. "The lake."

Daddy seemed to come to himself. Shook his head, then glanced at me. "That old man kept his dreams in here. All his crazy dreams of dead people."

"Like a diary?"

His voice rose. "Like a Book of the Dead."

When Daddy said the words, he made them ugly.

Not the way they sounded in my head. A Book of the Dead. Tender. Beautiful. Full of hope.

"This isn't for you," he said. "Now, eat your breakfast."

I stared into my father's eyes. "How did it get in the lake, Daddy?"

He stood and slid his chair under the table. "I . . . I got rid of it. Threw it out there. Years ago."

I nodded. Nodded.

"Grampa helped me find it. Yesterday."

Dad spun back to face me. "Listen here. I don't want you down to the lake again unless I am with you. It's dangerous. And this here book? It's not for a little girl."

"There ain't nothing in there anymore," I said. "It's been washed away."

The happiness of Momma was gone. The happiness from the book was gone, too. It was me and Daddy again. Butting heads. Neither one of us giving in.

"Good," he said. "It was malarkey. Now stay out of the water."

"Why?" I said. My bones grew stiff with rebellion.

"I done told you. You can't go down to the lake. It's dangerous." Daddy finished off his coffee and put the cup in the sink.

I stood, too, my fork dripping maple syrup onto the tablecloth, making the shape of a tiny penny. "You can't tell me not to go down there," I said. "I'm looking for something."

Daddy's voice was raw. "You will do as I say, young lady. And I am telling you *not* to go to the lake alone. I want to be with you if you're in that water. You hear me?"

"Yes, sir, I hear you." Then I shut my mouth tight, and I didn't look at Daddy again.

Two things nagged at me. First, I didn't dare say another word, lest he figure out I *would* be on my way to the lake before he was even out of the driveway. 'Course, I wouldn't be alone, thank goodness for Bobby.

But second, I could see Daddy knew something about the lake, too, even if he wasn't talking.

"Close as I can figure," I said, "that ledger came from a resting place."

Bobby didn't say nothing, just sat on the edge of the boat, tipping us a little to the side, staring at me. His mouth hung open.

I didn't look at him when I said the next words. "A resting place for the dead."

Wasn't nothing to be heard but the pat of the lake on the boat and, from far away, the call of a mockingbird.

"I see."

I peered into the water in the direction we had seen the lights the day before. "It seems it's a place *my* dead go. Or something like that."

"So there ain't no gold?" Bobby said.

I thought about that. "Not that you can pick up and hold."

"I kinda thought we was hunting for gold." Bobby's voice was low. Not mad. Confused sounding. "Bullion."

"I never said gold of any kind, Bobby," I said, staring off over his ear. "And that is the truth."

"Right. You said treasure."

It was time to tell him everything. He might walk away. Or row us away and set off on home. It scared me to think about what could happen.

But Bobby had a right to know.

I took in a deep breath. "We gotta talk, Bobby." This time I didn't look away.

Then I told him the whole story.

He nodded. Didn't ask many questions. At the end he said, "Seems awful far-fetched, Libby." He shaded his eyes with his hand, looking at me. "But possible."

"You think so?" I said, happy that he hadn't said "I gotta get outta here."

"Sure. Why not? You seen them pictures of the moon they been taking? If we can send cameras to the moon, why cain't we see people that's gone on?"

"I guess we can," I said. "I mean, I know *I* can."

"And what about *Star Trek?*"

"What about it?"

"You seen them Vulcans?"

I nodded. Gave me bad dreams, those Vulcans did.

"Somebody thought *that* was possible and now it is. Right?"

Again, I nodded.

"So why not what you're saying, Libby?" He shrugged.

"Yeah," I said. The sun beat down hot. "Why not?"

Chapter Fourteen

The water, warm as a bath, cooled as I went deeper. Toward the light. I looked back only once and saw the bottom of the boat, waving like it was saying good-bye.

I tugged on the rope me and Bobby had brought so he would know I was okay. The water felt fine on my skin, like I was meant to be here. Like maybe this here was a place for family.

Grampa's voice came into my head. Surprised filled me. I could hear him good, like he was with me. Like he was close enough to touch.

Terrific job, Libby, he said. *I knew you'd figure it out.*

Bobby tugged at the rope, and I pulled back.

"I'm okay," I said. The words floated up in fat air bubbles toward the surface where I watched them pop open. Had he heard me?

I squinted at the shimmer below.

Bobby tugged again, and I looked back over my shoulder toward the boat. It seemed miles away. The rope, like a cord to the surface, snaked down to me. I tugged back, watching as it coiled up to Bobby, taking the message that I was safe with it.

Had I thought my family might be here?

That they might visit like Grampa did?

That somehow they were underwater?

I wanted to see them all. Momma, Gramma, Daddy's brothers—kin I'd met and kin I'd never laid eyes on.

It was then I knew. The Lochewoods were here and on the shore and at the old family house. Our love was all over this place. Maybe all over Lake Mary.

Bobby tugged at the rope again. This time faster pulls, like he wanted to reel me in.

You have to go. Grampa's voice was in my ear, in my pounding head.

"I want to see Momma," I said, with an ache thick as wet sand. "Can't I see Momma before I go?"

There was no answer.

I rose with the bubbles.

When my head came through the water, and I dragged in air that almost burned, I found myself face-to-face with Daddy.

We left the boat on the far side of the lake. Daddy pointed for me and Bobby to get into the truck, and we did.

My father didn't say a word all the way home. But I could see them anyway. Could see them words waiting to come out of his mouth. He was so mad the veins in his neck throbbed.

We drove home fast. Bouncing over the sandy road around the lake. Crashing through the undergrowth that was tall enough in places to hide a house. Me and Bobby hitting into each other, Bobby holding on to my elbow like I could keep him safe. Until, at last, we were on the real road.

Then Daddy, lips still locked around all that he had to say, drove fast to Bobby's trailer.

Daddy dropped Bobby off. He didn't get a chance to say good-bye. Didn't even get to shut the door to the cab before Daddy tore away, making a U-turn there in the road and headed back home.

"What the Sam Hill were you thinking?"

Daddy stood in the living room, looking down at me. I sat in Grampa's chair, still wet, my knees pulled up to my chin. My hair drip drip dripped.

"What in the *Sam Hill* were you thinking?"

I could feel Daddy's fury, it was that hot.

He hadn't said a word till we got in the house. Then, like the winds from a hurricane, he started. He had been yelling a good ten minutes, and as far as I could tell, we weren't even close to the eye of the storm. I tried to slip in a word now and then, but it did me no good. Daddy might be asking questions, but he sure didn't want any answers.

"You said—"

"No! I told you not to go down there without me." Daddy clenched and unclenched his fists. "And you did what you wanted."

"I—"

"Have you ever seen anyone drown, girl?"

I wanted to say no, that I had almost done the drowning thing myself, but there wasn't the chance to get a word in edgewise.

"I have. When I was a kid." He thumped his chest with his finger. "My friend's brother drowned in a lake in Chuluota." Daddy paced in front of me. "Went down and didn't come up."

We sat quiet for some moments, Daddy back in time. When he spoke again, his voice was softer.

"Your grampa come driving in to get me. Saw what was going on. Saw all of us crying or screaming or standing there without a sound. He went into the water and found that boy."

I looked at Daddy over the tops of my knees. I thought of Grampa walking out into that lake. I could almost see him searching in the darkness of that water. Did he hold his breath? Was that lake different than ours?

"I waited in water up to my calves, along with lots of other people. All of us helpless. My friend's momma crying. His daddy sitting silent. Pop brought that boy, gray as a seal, out to the land and laid him down at their feet."

The whole thing played out in my head, and it near broke my heart. If I knew anything, I knew about losing someone.

I knew about being alone.

"We could see too much time had gone by."

Again Daddy was quiet. Sitting in the painful place memory sometimes lives. I wondered about that boy. What was *his* gift? Had he gone home afterwards to talk to his family? Had they listened?

Or had they been like my daddy?

Too stubborn to look?

"I'm real sorry—"

"Do not say anything, girl. Being sorry about doing what I told you not to do is easy when you're getting in trouble."

"What I was trying to say was I'm sorry about your friend's brother. I'm glad Grampa was there to help out."

"But what about what *you* did?"

I had a case of the nerves thinking about answering my father. I wanted to get up and move, to talk with my hands, to speak on my feet, but I was trapped in that ol' chair. "I know you don't get it—"

"What? Ain't you heard a word I said, girl?"

I nodded. "I heard."

Daddy was silent, taking in a breath for the next bout of yelling, no doubt.

Then he sunk to the floor in front of me, like he was taking a time-out to pray. He looked at me in a way he hadn't in forever. Like he saw me.

"Girl," he said, "what if you drowned out there? What if *you* died? What if *you* left me, too?"

I saw he cared in the creases around his eyes, in the sound of his voice. In the way he looked at me.

My heart grew as wide open as a sunflower.

I had answers aplenty, that was sure. But I couldn't very well say to him, "If you'd just believe Daddy, I could visit you if I died."

First off, I didn't want to die, visiting privileges or no.

It wasn't my time. And there was things to be done still. I knew that.

And truth was, too, I did not *want* to leave him.

Even if it meant getting to listen to Grampa play the guitar with all my uncles and my gramma.

Even if it meant seeing Momma again.

Even if he kept to his lonely self, I wanted to be with my daddy for as long as I could.

"I promise I won't drown, Daddy," I said, whispering.

Daddy's eyes filled up with tears. "Girl, you know I couldn't make it without you. You know we ain't whole if somebody's missing. And I am missing everyone but you."

I took in air. My hands trembled. It was plain Daddy did know some things. And that gave me a crumb of hope.

Maybe he would hear me out.

Maybe.

"Daddy?" I still whispered. "I have to tell you something. You have to know this, Daddy. I did what I had to do. I have to go to the lake. I *have* to."

My father bowed his head. I reached out and touched his blond hair. He needed a trim. When he was feeling better, not so mad at me, and if he'd let me, why I'd cut a few of those curls for him.

"No matter what you say, Daddy, I have to finish my work out there."

My voice settled near the floor.

He got to his feet.

"We'll see about that," he said.

Chapter Fifteen

I feel like I am getting close enough to touch whatever it is," I told Grampa, my heart still all wore out from my meeting with Daddy.

He nodded.

"Like that's it, right there." I pointed to nothing in the air in front of my face and then made a grab at it. I opened my empty hand to my grandfather.

"Libby?" Grampa said, and his breath came out in a cloud of light. "Listen. It'll get harder afore it gets easier."

"What do you mean, Grampa?" I took his hand in my own. It was no longer tough and worn, like it had been the day of his dying. Now it was smooth and young.

"The thing about belief is that it's hard to do some-times. You know that old saying 'Seeing is believing'?"

"Yes, sir."

"It's easier when you seen something to believe in it, right?"

I shrugged. "I guess so."

"But if you build up a wall against believing, seeing sometimes ain't enough."

"I think I get it," I said, remembering Daddy's telling of Momma coming to him after she passed. It sure would be nice to see her again. See that smile from the pictures.

"Thing is," Grampa said, "we all make deals before we are born on what we are going to do with our gifts. Part of our deal is we—those of us gone on—can't do nothing but encourage when the going is hard as nails."

"So you're saying I have to figure it all on my own?"

Grampa nodded, and I settled close to him, feeling the spark move through him and into me.

"But remember what you've heard. Remember the clues."

"I will," I said.

Grampa was quiet, then he said in a low voice, "We can't have you all alone, Libby."

"Why, I have you, Grampa. I have you and Daddy."

"Your daddy ain't nothing but a shell. He ain't who he used to be."

I stared at the light around Grampa. I knew that was true though I couldn't remember my father being whole my own self. I nodded then yawned. "Let's just sit here quiet for a while," I said. Tomorrow promised work, and I wanted to get as much comfort from Grampa as I could before I had to face the day.

I woke to Melinda Burls staring me in the face.

"What?" My voice came out like a scream. "What are you doing in here?" I pulled the sheet to my chin though I was dressed in a to-the-knees T-shirt.

"Just praying for ya," Preacher Burls said.

"Well, don't," I said.

She squeezed her eyes shut and moved her lips.

"I don't need that," I said. "I can pray good for my-self. And I do, too." I threw back the sheet and got out of bed. I went to the chest of drawers and grabbed some-thing clean to wear. Then I marched past the preacher and into the bathroom to get dressed.

Hadn't been in there two minutes when she tapped on the door.

"Libby, I got breakfast fixed up."

I looked to the crack at the bottom of the door. I could see the shadow of her feet. Good grief. "I'll be out in a minute."

"You know your daddy's been worried about you."

I changed my clothes quick and set to brushing my teeth.

"He asked me to stop in and stay with you."

Oh, great! "For how long?" I said through toothpaste foam. Bubbles landed on the mirror, but I didn't wipe them away.

"The day. Till he gets offen work."

"Don't you have church duties to perform? Sick people to visit? Someone to heal?"

"You are my church work today, Libby Lochewood." I imagined Melinda Burls smiling big in my face.

Now what was I going to do? I spit into the sink. The bathroom window was too small to crawl out of. I'd have to take my chances out *there*. With her. My babysitter. The Lake Mary Church of Christ preacher.

The preacher stood in the doorway when I tried to get out of the bathroom.

"You wash your hands?" she said.

I put my hands on my hips. "Did you know," I said, "my birthday is September 28? I will be thirteen. Very near a woman."

She smiled.

"Just so's you know," I said, "I don't need anyone here watching over me."

We stood face-to-face in the hall, light coming in from

my room and Daddy's room and the kitchen. Squares of sunlight meeting here in the center of the house and falling all around us.

I had never stood like this with any preacher before, 'specially not this one. Always kinda watched her from a distance, even when she was in our house. Watched her with the congregation, watched her leading and singing and praying, watched her with my daddy. I had never seen how clear the blue of her eyes were. Had never noticed that she had smile lines coming up real faint from her lips, and that her skin had a just-powdered look.

"Did you wash your hands?" she said again.

"No." I went back into the bathroom, grabbed the soap, and lathered up.

"Let's go eat," she said when I was done.

She followed wherever I went. Even to the phone when I called Bobby.

"Do you mind?" I said, holding the phone to my shoulder.

"Not at all," she said, and kept standing there, her arms crossed over her thin chest.

"I mean, will you let me speak in private?"

She moved four steps back.

I waved a hand at her, to shoo her even farther away, but Preacher Burls was determined to please my daddy.

"Bobby," I said when he was on the phone.

"Hey, Libby."

"Meet me at the usual place."

There was a pause.

"What?" I said.

"Your daddy come by this morning. He talked to my mama, and she ain't allowing me to step one foot off the property."

My stomach landed in my heels.

"So you ain't coming?" I turned away from Preacher Burls and kept my voice a whisper.

"I can't get away," he said. I could hear the sorrow in his voice, and I knew I wouldn't be seeing him today.

"I better go then." I hung up before Bobby could hear me cry.

There I stood in the hall, by our green telephone, and willed the tears back where they come from.

Melinda Burls cleared her throat. "You wanna read the Bible this morning?"

I went to my room and wept there.

She didn't nap. She didn't watch TV. She didn't pick up even one book other than the Bible. Daddy was gonna have to pay her double for being such a good babysitter.

I met my father on the front porch that evening.

"You know what, Daddy?" I said as he came inside, his plaid shirt dirty from work. The screen door closed with a *pop*. "You double-crossed me."

Daddy glanced in my general direction. Why, he didn't even have the guts for full eye contact! Just like always. From inside the house came the smell of roasted chicken and homemade rolls. I knew from all the shredding of cabbage and carrots I had done we'd also be eating coleslaw.

"Daddy," I said.

"What, girl?" He gave me an almost look then peered around me. Maybe he was checking to see if the babysitter was still here. She was.

I wasn't quite sure what to say to him. Outside the sun sunk slow into the west. The whole of our land was colored orange.

"Listen." I leaned on my tiptoes toward him, my hands planted on my hips. "School ain't but a few more days away from starting, Daddy."

"I know that."

"And I have much to accomplish before I get to going there full-time."

Daddy let air out of his lungs like a popped balloon. "What is it that you have to do?"

"You do not take me serious," I said. "What I have to say matters more to me than anything I have ever told you. Every time I try to talk to you about the dead, you excuse me. Or you yell. Or you point your finger at me like I am a little girl still. And, Daddy, I am not. I am going on thirteen. This month to be exact, though *you* may not remember. I want you to know that this was my grandfather that went on, not just your daddy. He was my very best friend in the whole wide world."

"Do you know," Daddy said. He went to point at me but scratched at his head instead. "Do you know how long I been listening to these outrageous stories about the dead? I am sick and tired of them."

I was sucking in air to proceed with my argument when Preacher Burls said, "What stories of the dead?"

Chapter Sixteen

Well, Grampa," I said, "she is a half-believer."

"Always thought she was, the way she talked at church and all."

I knelt on the bed beside him, my arms wrapped around him, my head resting on his shoulder. Holding onto Grampa was like taking in the sweetest drink ever. Only all that goodness went in through my pores and straight to my heart where it seemed to give me strength.

We sat quiet a long time. Then Grampa said, "Libby. I don't want to talk too soon, but I think you are making some terrific progress with your daddy."

"You do?" Warmth filled me up to my eyebrows. I grinned. "You told me it would get harder first."

"It will," Grampa said. "But you are doing the right things."

"I sure hope so. I have made it my one goal to accomplish before the summer is done."

"Bringing in Burls was a right smart idea."

"I didn't do that on my own, Grampa. She came into it herself. She's real nosy that way."

When I told Preacher Melinda Burls some of what I had to do—about helping the living and the dead get connected—she stared at Daddy and said, "Why, Earl? Why're you doubting? It says straight up in the scriptures that after Jesus was resurrected that many of them who slept was seen again. It *is* possible, Earl."

"Near a lake, Melinda?" Daddy had said. "They was seen near a lake?"

"She was the one convinced him to let me try, Grampa. For us all to go out there together."

"I know," he said. His smile was like the sunrise. Made my eyes hurt.

"Daddy sure was surprised." I giggled, and Grampa laughed low in his chest.

When I woke up the next morning, I was still smiling.

Melinda Burls picked up Bobby and brought him to our house. She promised us a huge breakfast once we got back home 'cause everyone knows you got to wait a hour after you eat to go into the water. Then we headed off.

Daddy drove all four of us around to the opposite side of the lake where we had left the boat. He grumbled the whole way.

"If you want, Libby," Melinda Burls said, squished between me and Daddy, with poor Bobby pressed against the door handle, "I can take you school shopping next week. Your daddy says you need some things."

"Oh?" A dash of regret hit me in the chest. Never again, in this lifetime, would I be able to go to the Kmart with Grampa and get me stuff for school. The thought stung. Made my throat burn.

I glanced out the side window, past Bobby. The trees and bushes of our land sped by. We would be to the lake in no time. "Maybe," I said. "Maybe that'd be all right." I didn't mean it.

She was just doing what Daddy asked, so he didn't have to, but there was still lots of things to Grampa's death that were gonna take some getting used to.

We bounced along the sand road, the windows rolled down, the heat of the day pressing in on us. Though it wasn't that late, a storm threatened. At last we were to where we had left the boat two days before.

"We shoulda been stealing the truck," I said to Bobby, low, so Daddy wouldn't hear. "Sure is a lot faster than rowing all the way over here."

"I was thinking that same thing," Bobby said, and he grinned in my face, showing me that chipped-off tooth of his. "I can drive, you know. Read about how in the newspaper."

Daddy stopped us with a jerk, and we climbed out of the cab—unhappy all over his face. A breeze cooled me off some.

"Now what?" Daddy said. He squinted out over the water. His blond hair looked like a white halo. I blinked, and the halo was gone.

"We know where to go," Bobby said. He pulled at the boat that sat half in, half out of the water. Frogs called out, telling us to get on outta here, then going silent when we got too close.

"Watch out for snakes," Melinda Burls said. She bit at her nails. "I hate snakes. They are God's most lowly creatures. They are Satan."

"Plenty of snakes out here," Bobby said. "My daddy always tells me that. He says Florida equals snakes."

"Shh, now," she said and shivered.

Daddy let out a unhappy laugh.

Me and Melinda Burls got in the boat. It tipped hard to the right, and for a moment I thought she would pitch into the three-foot-deep water. She sat down quick. Daddy and Bobby climbed in the boat next. Bobby took the oars.

"This is my job," he said, jabbing at the sand and pushing us out deeper.

It didn't take us anytime at all to get to the place from this side of the lake. A few good strokes, and we were headed in the right direction.

"Gotta make this quick," Daddy said. "I got work to do." He looked at the sun like it was his watch. Two red-winged blackbirds balanced on the cattails.

"We're almost there," I said. I looked to the direction of the spring, ignoring my father. The light splashed on the lake, setting my eyes on edge, blinding me.

"Now I know," Melinda Burls said like she was preaching in church, "that there are snakes in that there part of the water." She gave a half-hearted point. Like she was worried if she stuck her hand out too far, a snake would get her finger.

"We're safe in the boat," Daddy said.

"I'm not so sure," Bobby said. He never stopped rowing.

We all looked at him.

"And why is that?" Melinda Burls said.

"My momma told me a story of a man who was out

in his boat, fishing, when snakes—moccasins—attacked the craft. She read it in the newspaper."

I made cutting motions at my throat for Bobby to stop talking.

Melinda Burls let out a gasp. Daddy seemed more-than-usual put out.

Wasn't nothing I could do to stop Bobby. I knew that. I rested back to hear the story.

Bobby let a big pause of silence into the air.

"What happened?" Melinda Burls said. Her voice sounded like it came from under the boat. Her hands searched for the beads that she wasn't wearing. She settled for gripping the collar of her psychedelic *Jesus Is My Lord* T-shirt.

"A few days later, some other fishermen come out on the river. Saw that boat. Knew there was a all-points bulletin out for a missing fisherman."

Now I rolled my eyes. "Why didn't the policemen go looking on the river theirselves? I mean, if that was the last place he was seen, wouldn't the police have checked for him there?"

Bobby slapped at the air like my words were gnats. "Anyways, they seen the boat. Paddled over to it. And there was the guy. Three days he'd been laying in the sun. His face was the color of a beet—you know, dark purple-ish?—and swolled up the size of a melon."

"What kind a melon?" I said, like I was interested. "Mush or water?"

Melinda Burls looked from me to Bobby. Her eyes and lips were tight lines.

Daddy stared at my friend like he was nutty.

"Cantaloupe," Bobby said. "But there's more. He was dead as a old boot. Bite marks all over him. And when the policemen—here's the police part, Libby—when the policemen tried to move the dead guy? A mess a nesting moccasins swarmed them."

Melinda let out a gasp like she might faint.

Daddy cleared his throat. "Why, thank you, Bobby," he said, "for starting out our day so pretty."

"Here we are," Bobby said. He held the oars straight in the water so the boat would slow its course. He threw the cement block overboard.

Daddy, who sat knee-to-knee with Melinda Burls, said, "Now what, girl?"

"Now we go in," I said.

"Into the water?" Melinda said.

I nodded. "Of course."

"If you go deep enough," Bobby said, "you can see the lights for yourself. It's pretty cool."

Again I nodded.

"You seen 'em?" Daddy said.

"Yes, sir." Bobby gazed at Daddy.

"My girl talked you into it?"

Bobby shook his head. "No, sir. I seen the stuff long before she had something to say."

Daddy looked away.

"I don't swim that good," Melinda Burls said. She tugged on the collar of her shirt.

"What?" I said, feeling all kinds of surprised. "You're always going in lakes and swimming pools and rivers to baptize people." I had been baptized in Crystal Lake right here in Lake Mary. "And you can't swim?"

"I dog-paddle." She bit at her lip. "Don't have to go out too deep if you're baptizing someone. Just gotta get them under all the way is all. You could do that in a bath-tub, but it's a bit awkward."

"My goodness," I said. "A Florida girl ought to know how to swim."

She looked at me, her eyes matching the blue of the sky above, and said nothing.

"I can swim," Daddy said. He spoke with his no-sass-ain't-standing-for-no-malarkey voice. "So I'll go down."

I stood, rocking the boat some. "I'll go with you."

"No, you won't," Daddy said. He didn't wait for an answer. Just stepped over into the water. His head bobbed up, he caught some air, and went under.

Bobby stared after my father. "He ain't gonna see nothing," he said, his voice almost a whisper.

A knot of tears snarled in the back of my throat, making it hard to talk. "And why is that, Mister Know-It-All?" Anger and pain slugged away at those tears, trying to keep them from falling, but a little of the hurt came out my mouth and aimed itself at Bobby.

"'Cause he don't believe he will." Bobby stared at me, like he was trying to prepare me for the worst or something.

What? I wanted to say. I wanted to say, *How did you know that, Bobby Myers?* But I didn't say anything 'cause I knew he was right about Daddy. And goodness, that knowing? It stabbed me straight to the core.

"Should we worry about him?" Preacher Burls said. She chewed at a nail. "Should we pray?"

"Nah," Bobby said. "Here he comes."

The first words out of Daddy's mouth was, "We can go on home. There ain't nothing in that water except fish and sunlight and the bottom."

"Are you sure?" Melinda Burls peered over the edge. Her fingertips went white, the way she gripped the side of the boat.

"Did you stay under the shadow of the boat?" Bobby said. "That helps you see easier."

"There wasn't nothing there," Daddy said and hefted himself up, tipping us all toward him.

I cried then. Didn't even try to stop the tears. "But you saw the light."

"*Sun*light," Daddy said and ran his hand over his face like a washrag.

This was my last chance. I'm not sure how I knew that. But if Gramma and Grampa couldn't convince Daddy. If I couldn't. If this small boatload of people couldn't get him to believe even a little, well then, everything was lost. Who knew what that meant for Grampa? For my family?

For me and Daddy?

Daddy sat on the bottom of the boat, dripping the lake all around him. We all stared at each other.

"What are you crying about, girl?" Daddy said.

What could I say?

"Storm coming." Melinda glanced at the sky. In baby steps it turned the color of early evening.

"Let's get on home then," Daddy said. He smacked his hands together, making that stinging sound wet hands make. "Storm's almost here."

Bobby sat still. "Libby?" he said. When I didn't move, he pulled the block up out of the water.

I stood.

"Girl?" Daddy said.

"You won't believe," I said. "You won't even try."

"Don't you yell at me, girl," Daddy said.

"You are scared. Scareder than anyone I ever met."

"Hush now, Libby." Melinda Burls's mouth dropped open wide enough to catch a family of crawfish. "That ain't respectful."

"You're chicken guts."

"Oops," Bobby said.

The boat rocked with all my words pouring outta me.

"You could see if you would look. Momma already tried to contact you, but you pushed her away."

Daddy got to his feet so we were sorta eye to eye. "I don't even know what you are talking about."

"You told me yourself," I said, my voice so loud I heard it run off across the lake in the direction of our home. "You told me she came in the room like an angel and that you told her—"

"That was a dream, girl."

"Naw, it wasn't Daddy. It was her. Coming to see you. Coming to fix the hole in the family."

"I don't know what you are talking about," Daddy said again. Overhead, the sky darkened, sunk toward us.

"Yes, you do," I said. "You're afraid."

I saw I was dead-on. He *was* scared. But I didn't have time for that.

"Libby," Melinda Burls said. "Sit down, please and thank you. It's raining."

And it was. Drops like dimes fell from the sky.

"Libby?" Bobby said.

"Let's get on home," Daddy said, soft, in my face. He reached to touch my arm.

But I jerked away from him. Then I leaped into the lake.

Water closed around my head, bubbles chattering as they rose. I could hear Daddy's voice above me though I couldn't make out the words.

I looked for the lights. And there they were. Right where they were supposed to be. The cement block sunk past—someone must have let it out again—and a few fishes darted away. I took off, to the edge of the light.

Chapter Seventeen

I heard the plunge behind me. *Good ol' Bobby,* I thought.

But no. It was my father. Arrowing into the water with his dive. A large air bubble coming from one nose hole.

Daddy? I was surprised. I motioned to my father. *Come this way.* I waved to him, and he swam to me, his eyes open. His face mad. He pointed to the surface.

Grampa was in my head. In my mind, his smile lit the whole of the water around me, like he was a star, all himself.

I turned back to my father, who made to grab at me.

Daddy took a hold of my arm, but I moved away

from him. Swam toward the light. He followed, angry. Gripped my arm. Pulled me toward the surface.

We crashed into the air. "Let go!" I said.

And then . . .

"Libby?"

I saw her standing on the shore. Standing behind Grampa. My mother. Oh, my mother. It felt like my heart melted at the sight of her. I hadn't realized I missed her so much.

"Momma?"

"What?" Daddy said. He looked in the direction I did.

She came toward me, stepping into the lake, calling my name. And in her arms was a baby, small as could be. "Libby," she said. "Oh, Libby. I have waited for this moment."

My body took over, and I swam toward her. Closer.

She waded knee-deep into the water, reached out. It felt like her hand drifted across my cheek. She pressed her lips to my face.

I saw her see Daddy, who almost growled in my ear. "Get on into that boat, girl. We gotta get back to shore."

"Earl?" Momma said. She handed the baby to my grandfather.

Those baby eyes opened. Her lips puckered.

"Who is this, Grampa?" I said, but I knew before

he answered. This here was my sister. Unborn when Momma died.

"You were gonna have a baby," I said, surprise making me rise some in the water.

Me and Daddy were treading at the lake. His eyes grew round as tangerines.

"When Momma died, there was supposed to be a baby girl. A sister for me."

"How did you know that?" Daddy took hold of my shoulder. "How did you—"

Momma grasped Daddy's arm.

He looked to where her hand rested. Had he felt the electricity of it? Overhead, lightning sparked.

"Wait, Emily," Grampa said. He was beside Momma without even moving. Like a thought. "He doesn't believe yet."

"He has to believe," Momma said. Her face was young as a teenager's. Her hair long, past her waist, moving like seaweed. The dress she wore floated with the lake, like the hem of it danced on its own to a slow song. "We're not whole without him. We're not complete."

"You know he must come to it on his own," Grampa said.

"I miss him," Momma said. She whispered in his ear, "I miss you, Earl."

All this time Daddy still looked to where Momma's hand was.

"Let him go, Emily," Grampa said. "He can't stay in this water. If he dies, our Libby will be all alone. She'll have no one."

Could Daddy die here, now? Drown? I knew the answer without thinking more than the question. "Momma," I said. "Please let Daddy go."

When Momma wailed, Daddy looked right at me. "What is that?" he said. Then, my daddy, he started to sink.

I let out a scream.

Bobby said, "What, Libby?"

Preacher Burls said, "Earl! You get on back into this here boat."

But Daddy sunk further into the water till his head was submerged. And when I tried to pull him back, he slipped through my fingers. Down, down, down he went, like he was the anchor.

Then Grampa was there. Lifting Daddy to air the way he had with me my first time. Even though I didn't need it—'cause I believed. It was clear to me now, as I watched them. An unbeliever would drown. An unbeliever had no faith.

Grampa pushed Daddy up to the boat. Up to the air

where Melinda Burls and Bobby worked to get my father aboard.

All around me was screaming and crying from both the living and the dead and the comforting sounds a new baby makes. I couldn't tell where any of it came from. But as I swam to where my father was, going no faster than bubbles, I saw that my sister looked just like him.

When I looked back over my shoulder, my whole family was gone.

"He ain't breathing," Melinda Burls screamed. Her voice went out all over the lake. "He ain't breathing."

Rain slammed us. Bobby pulled Daddy to the side of the boat. I waited for the water to pour out of him, like it had from me.

But that didn't happen. It didn't happen because my father was not a believer.

Fear thick as a telephone line traveled through my veins. I pushed Daddy from below. He was so heavy I almost couldn't move him up higher.

"He ain't breathing!" Melinda Burls spoke to heaven.

"Libby," Bobby said. "What do we do?" I could hear how scared he was. Scared as I felt, maybe.

Somehow we got Daddy out of the water. He was too tall to lie flat in the boat. His knees bent over the wooden seat. Water spread out all around him. It was like we sat in the rain cloud.

Bobby was talking, but I couldn't understand a thing he said. Just heard the pounding of my own blood.

Preacher Burls, her mouth working in prayer, grabbed Daddy around the shoulders, pulled him to her chest in a hug. She hit him on the back over and over. Hit him in the chest.

I kicked my way into the boat, the wood biting my hip bones.

Bobby struck at my father's legs, tears running down his face.

"Daddy?" The lake spilled out of my mouth. I clutched my father's arms and jerked him away from Melinda Burls till he sat up. His eyes were open but not seeing a thing. He was as gray as the clouds we sat in. *What good is it having a preacher with us?* I thought, though it didn't even make sense when the words popped into my mind.

"No, no, no," I said.

Bobby pounded on Daddy's thighs. "Breathe," he shouted. "Breathe."

Melinda Burls rocked Daddy back from me. She spoke at the sky, but it only answered with rain that splattered the boat.

He was gone.

My daddy was gone.

I was alone.

"Daddy?" I said. Then, "Make him breathe."

I looked over the side of the boat, and there I saw my grandfather. He stood with my father. Daddy held his baby in one arm and my mother in the other. He kissed her forehead.

I slapped at the surface of the lake. Daddy looked at me, and I saw him say *Libby*. His eyebrows moved together like he worried.

Behind me, Melinda Burls cried out to heaven.

Libby.

Libby.

"Libby?" Now I heard him say my name.

He said my name.

I swished my hand toward him. There was no one in the lake. No one on the shore. No one.

It was just me and my daddy and I could not do this without him. I could not do it all alone. Lochewoods were family. We were supposed to be together forever. Families were supposed to be together forever.

Bobby grabbed me tight around the waist. He was bawling. "Libby," he said.

"Libby," Daddy said again.

"Thank you," Melinda said behind me. And when I looked back in the boat, I saw Daddy reaching for my hand. Alive.

I crawled to my father. The rain fell hard, then harder. And then it was gone. Just the dark clouds were left.

"Libby," Daddy said, like his throat hurt him to speak. "Libby, I seen them all standing right where your momma and me was gonna build our own house."

"You did, Daddy?"

He nodded. "I did."

Chapter Eighteen

Things changed.

First off, Daddy began living again. I mean, he wasn't unhappy any more. He whistled, something I couldn't remember my whole life, except on the bare edges of when I was a little ol' thing.

And he smiled. All the time.

The whole house changed for us because Daddy could smile again.

"I know we keep on going," he said to me one evening, when he was fresh from the groves and it was just me and him sitting on the porch, watching the fireflies. The whole backyard was alive with them.

"Nice thing to know, ain't it?" I pulled my knees up and wrapped my arms around them. School started in two days, and I had clothes shopping to do.

Daddy cleared his throat then looked at me side-eyed. "Libby, you was right all along, and I am sorry I fought you so hard. Wished I had acted different when Pop was around. Sure would have made life easier. For all of us."

I thought of Daddy, worn thin before. And how now, even when he didn't smile, his face seemed to be grinning like all get out.

That's what knowing we are forever did for him. And I was real glad I could oblige him by helping out some.

"Libby?"

I sat straight up in bed. Grampa was there, light spreading out around him as he moved near to where I was.

"Hey, Grampa," I said.

He sat next to me, and I pulled over close. The smell of honey came at me, strong and sweet.

"Listen, Libby girl," he said. "I got to tell you something."

"What's that, Grampa?"

He was quiet a moment, then he said, "First off, let me tell you if'n you hadn't gotten your daddy to believe, well, Libby, the family circle never would have been complete. A family ain't whole if it ain't together. No matter what it looks like. Only a momma and a daddy. Or a daddy and his girl. Or something as big as what we got."

I nodded.

"You done real good work." He looked toward Daddy's room.

Joy spread all through me. I felt it all the way to the ends of my hair.

"What is it, Grampa?" I said. "You're leading up to something."

Grampa fidgeted, light swelling and rolling like waves.

"You soothed things over for us, Libby," he said. "And now you got other work to do."

I sat still. "What do you mean 'other work'? I can't think of anything more than what's happened that's important."

"You got that right, baby girl," Grampa said. "But it's like this. You got *living* to do. And your daddy, he does, too. Living ain't got that much to do with us who's gone on."

I kept quiet. Then, "What're you saying, Grampa?" Cold water splashed all over me. "Wait—you mean you ain't coming back?"

"Not so much. Not like when I been needing to help you and your daddy."

I almost dropped my teeth on the floor. "But you said . . ." I couldn't even think. Words floated in my brain, and I had to grab at the right ones to make sense. "You said you'd always be here for me."

Grampa nodded and light splashed on the opposite wall.

"I will be," he said. "When you need us most, any one of us will be here. The whole circle of us will be here if you need us bad. If you have something to talk over that can't wait."

Without meaning to, I started to cry. "Well, I need you," I said. "I need you right now and I will tomorrow and the next day and the next. The dead—" I took in a deep breath and wiped away tears. "The dead ain't never that far from the living. That's what you said, Grampa."

"We ease you through the pain," Grampa said, and his voice was low and honey-smelling. "That's part of my duties. I did that, didn't I?"

I thought all the way back to Grampa's falling on the floor. And that first night he had dropped in to visit me. It seemed like ages ago. Years and years. I remembered how good I felt knowing he was there for me. He *had* eased the way. He had done what he was supposed to. But I still didn't want him to go.

"I got school shopping to do," I said. "Homework. And later . . ." My mind filled up fast of all the things I'd be doing without my grandfather. There was a world of it waiting. High school. Dating. One day getting married, even. I didn't want to do that all alone. I needed to do it with friends and family. I needed *my grandfather* to be around.

"Libby," Grampa said, and he touched my hand, causing a spark to light up my knuckle. "I'll be back. Just not every night. Listen, Libby. If we're always hanging around, do you think Earl would stay in this world? I mean—he has the grove to take care of. He has the rest of his life." Grampa paused. "He has you."

A part of me felt like a baby. I wanted to throw myself on the floor. To scream. To kick. To thump my fists near my grandfather's feet.

"You helped your daddy to change," Grampa said. "It's like he's come back to life. He's here for you now. We couldn't leave you all alone. Not with him like that. Now you have someone here, too. Not just on the other side watching out for you. Now you got your daddy."

I hiccupped from crying so hard. "I can't do it alone. The dead's supposed to stay close to the living."

Grampa pulled me into a hug. His face was clear of wrinkles. His hands smooth. His hair fair as Daddy's. "We'll be near," he said. "Always. I promise."

That night when Grampa left I cried for what seemed hours. I thought things over for a good long time, too. Worrying. Maybe I had worked too fast. Figured things out too early. Why, all this was near as bad as when Grampa died and I thought I wouldn't see him again.

Okay, not really. But the truth was I had come to rely on his being with me even though he'd gone on. Now what?

I burst into fresh tears.

"Libby?" Daddy stood in the doorway. "I heard you crying, girl, so I come to check on you."

My daddy come to check on me. It took my breath away.

"He won't be back so much," I said. "Grampa done told me."

Daddy walked to the side of my bed and knelt by where I lay. He pressed his cool lips to my forehead, and I wrapped my arms around his neck.

"What am I going to do? I'm gonna be all alone now."

Daddy was quiet a few moments, then he said, "Why, I'm here for you, Libby." His voice was soft. "We ain't alone no more 'cause we have each other."

"Oh, Daddy," I said.

He sat on the edge of my bed for some time then, and we talked. We talked about the Sight, about family members gone on, and how me and him were together till it was all said and done.

Then Daddy said, "You know, Libby, you changed history in our family. You did what no one else could, girl. You showed me how to live."

"Naw, Daddy," I said. I wiped at my tears. "You had to believe on your own. I was here to just help you some."

Melinda Burls would have agreed with me. We find our faith and stick to it for better or for worse, she'd say. Sometimes it takes searching to get at the treasure.

"Get some sleep, girl," Daddy said when the morning sun lit up our world. "You ain't gonna be good for nothing if you don't rest."

Daddy left the room, and I heard him getting ready to go out to the groves. And as I went off to sleep, I realized something.

Sure, the dead ain't never that far from the living. My grampa had proved that. But I knew, too, in a strong family, that the living ain't never that far from the living. That was the treasure Grampa had left for me. Knowing that.

It's what keeps a family whole.

The day before school started I went shopping to the Kmart with Melinda Burls and Daddy. We had us a fine time. I got me underwear, including a real bra, four dresses, two skirts with matching shirts, and a new pair of shoes, too.

Red Keds. Just the right size.

Acknowledgments

A million years ago—or maybe it was a million and one years ago—I awoke from a dream where a friend of mine, Vivian Milius, was walking out of a Florida lake. Water fell from her hair and skin and clothing. She was filled with joy and content with who she was. That image sparked a book idea, and I started writing *Never That Far*.

Richard Peck looked over the first two pages of the story. "You haven't started in the right place," he said. "Is this the best first line?" I looked over the page, chopped the opening sentence, and started with the second. "You are no better than your first line," Richard says, and I believe that.

ACKNOWLEDGMENTS

I have several writer friends I trust to help me as I begin a creative work. My first readers were patient as I tried to figure out what was hidden in the lake. If the gift was real or ghostly. I'd like to thank Cheri Pray Earl (who has read too many drafts of too many books of mine), Chris Crowe (who said, "This novel is getting boring." I ignored him. A little.), and John Bennion (brilliant with his critiques). Rick Walton said what he always said to me, "Keep going, Carol."

Those weren't the only eyeballs roaming over the manuscript (how do you like *that* visual?). Ann Edwards Cannon and Louise Plummer both read through the book. These women are my mentors, and I love them dearly. Ann Dee Ellis read for me (and since then, she and I have written one and a half novels together). Then there was Lisa Hale and Kerry Spencer, who both were generous with their comments. And when I felt like the book was a gasping fish, taking its last breaths, Alane Ferguson read the book in one sitting. She was filled with praise and, like Rick, gave me the hope to keep working.

And so I did.

A million years later—or maybe a million and one— I got the distinct feeling that an editor named Lisa Mangum might like this novel. That thought nudged me and nudged me. Finally, I decided to listen and sent her a copy. Lisa did like the story, and I thank her for being a perfect editor, knowing what needed changing and knowing how to guide me to those changes. Any smart writer knows a terrific editor makes a good book a great book.

My agent, Stephen Fraser, Chris Schoebinger, and the skilled Jennifer De Chiara all worked together to finalize book details. To say these three people have my trust is an understatement. I am blessed to have them in my corner.

Finally, of course, I owe a big thank you to each of my daughters. Elise, Laura, Kyra, Caitlynne, and Carolina love what I write and cheer for me until they are hoarse. When I am gone, I plan to visit them, each one, at 2:35 in the morning. Until that day, they will continue to be the ones I read lines to while the ink is still wet.

Discussion Questions

1. One of Libby's best friends is her grandfather. What is your relationship like with your grandparents? Do you live near them? What do you admire about them?

2. Grampa tells Libby that "the dead are never that far from the living." What do you think he meant by that? Do you have people in your family who have passed away but who you still feel close to?

3. Libby accepts help from Bobby and Martha in order to find the treasure in the lake. What is her relationship like with Bobby? With Martha? Do you think Bobby and Martha really believe there is a treasure in the lake?

4. Libby's father is sad after Grampa dies. What were some of the things that Libby did that helped cheer him up? What are some things you could do to help a friend who is sad?

5. Where you surprised that the treasure in the lake was a book? What did you think it was going to be? Why was the book important to Libby and her family?

6. Families come in lots of different ways. Grampa even tells Libby that "A family ain't whole if it ain't together. No matter what it looks like. Only a momma and a daddy. Or a daddy and his girl. Or something as big as what we got." What does your family look like? What are some activities you like to do with your family?

7. If you had the gift of "Sight" and could see family members who have died, who would you want to see and why? What would you ask them?

8. Libby sneaks away to the lake even though her dad tells her not to go. Have you ever done something your parents told you not to do? Is it ever okay to disobey your parents? Why?

9. Libby was brave when she decided to swim to the bottom of the lake to look for the treasure. Share a time when you were brave.

10. Libby loves swimming in the lake and walking the land around her home. Describe a place you love to go. Use all five senses in your description.